POINT BREEZE STORIES

PAUL F. KENNEDY

Print ISBN: 978-1-54398-334-0

eBook ISBN: 978-1-54398-335-7

STORIES

ACKNOWLEDGEMENTS

I FIRST THANK my wife Patty, without whose love and support none of this would be possible. I thank my parents Paul and Marilou Kennedy, two of the many patriarchs and matriarchs of Point Breeze who formed us and guided us, and were the backbone of the neighborhood. Special thanks to my sister Marilyn for help with photography and creative design. Special thanks also to my sister Nancy for editing and writing advice. My siblings Kathi, Virginia, Mike, Bobby, Joan, and Mary were and are an integral part of my life's experience, and contributed to this work in ways they might not even realize. Thanks to Bruno Battistoli and Peter Blair – both life-long friends and fellow writers – for writing advice. Thanks to Ron Fuchs, Rocky Kalas, Joe Kennedy, Butch Blakeley, and Tim Conn. May I never forget my brilliant and talented grandmother Catherine Wise Bulger, who inspired me to become a writer. She's been gone for over thirty years, but her grandchildren still refer to her as Catherine the Great.

DISCLAIMER

THE TWO MEMOIRS in this collection, "Rite of Passage" and "Carl's Crew," are true stories. The fourteen short stories are fiction. Some of the characters depicted resemble real persons, living or dead, but are not identical and are in some cases composites. All plots are fictional. Two short stories, "Heroes" and "Blood Brothers," are narrated in the first person, but the narrator is a fictional boy of the neighborhood, not me. The memoirs and stories form a mosaic of a beautiful place, Point Breeze.

"Rite of Passage" was previously published in the *Pittsburgh Quarterly*. "Blood Brothers" was published by *Loyalhanna Review*. "The Rose of Kerry" was published by *Bridge and Tunnel Books*.

DEDICATION

THIS BOOK IS dedicated to the Point Breeze contemporaries of mine who died far too young. Sadly, there are too many to name, but I will mention several who were at one time close friends: Bill Natali, Chris Pahel, Mike McGinley, Steve Blair, and Kirk Curilla. The shared bond of time and place can never die.

AUTHOR BIOGRAPHY

PAUL F. KENNEDY lives in Aspinwall, PA with his wife Patty. He is a life-long Pittsburgher, born in Lawrenceville and reared in Point Breeze from age 2. He is a graduate of Central Catholic High School, Indiana University of Pennsylvania, and the Heinz School of Public Policy at Carnegie Mellon University (Master of Public Management.) He is a retired state disability hearing officer, and has been a free lance writer since the early 1990s. He is currently a docent at the Fort Pitt Block House museum and a cantor solo-ist at St. Scholastica Church. Hobbies include winemaking, travel, geneal-ogy, and studying languages.

Paul has written over 60 articles for the *Pittsburgh Tribune Review*, mostly about local history, including a 1997 feature article on the Point Breeze neighborhood. He has had poems published in *Laurel Highlands Scene, Raystown Review*, and *Miraculous Medal*. He has had short sto-ries published in *Bridge and Tunnel Books* and *Loyalhanna Review,* and a memoir in *Pittsburgh Quarterly*. He is the author of *A Pittsburgh Gamble*, a novel set in Pittsburgh at the time of the 1960 World Series, and of *Billy Conn: the Pittsburgh Kid,* a biography of Pittsburgh boxer Billy Conn. His 2014 article *The Man Who Saved the Block House* was featured on the front page of the Sunday *Post-Gazette* editorial section.

PRAISE FOR *POINT BREEZE STORIES*

"WHEN I READ these stories by Paul Kennedy, I'm in the thrall of an artful, Irish storyteller, regaling the reader with tales of Pittsburgh both old and new. He wonderfully recreates the Point Breeze neighborhood he grew up in as well as the wider city that encompasses it. Adroitly combining history and fiction, Kennedy makes us see and feel our past again: the families, fields, churches, and gravestones."

Peter Blair, Ph.D., University Writing Program, University of North Carolina – Charlotte

"Paul Kennedy is much more than a terrific storyteller. He is also a magician. How else to explain how he weaves fact and fiction, history and imagination into a lovely tapestry of characters and settings? For all their differences, all Pittsburgh neighborhoods are basically alike: great characters, some big and some small, some important and some seemingly innocuous, but all with their own stories to tell. And no one tells them better than Paul Kennedy. If you're a native "Yinzer" like me, you will love Point Breeze Stories. If not, by the time you finish this wonderful collection, you'll want to be."

Len Pasquarelli, retired sports journalist, 2008 inductee into the Pro Football Hall of Fame writers' wing and, most proudly, a native Pittsburgher.

BOOK SUMMARY

THIS COLLECTION OF fourteen fictional stories and two memoirs spans the time period from America's frontier days to the 21st century. All are set, at least in part, in the small neighborhood of Point Breeze, in the East End of Pittsburgh.

Baptism of Desire follows an Irish settler family in the 1700s caught in the struggle between British, French, and Native people for western Pennsylvania. They ultimately settle in what is now Point Breeze. Subsequent stories unfold during the disastrous 1877 railroad strike, the violent Prohibition era, and the Vietnam War. But most of the stories occur in the 1950s and 60s Baby Boom, when the author grew up in the neighborhood.

Many colorful characters populate these pages, but the real star is the neighborhood itself. Anyone who has ever lived or "loafed" in Point Breeze in the latter half of the twentieth century can relate well to these stories, but they are for all readers. The rich history of the past morphs into the raucous, kid-crowded mid-twentieth century and beyond. Tears of grief, joy, and nostalgia drip from the pages.

The collection concludes with two tender, poignant, and funny "coming of age" memoirs. It is the author's hymn to his home, his history, his people.

MEMORIES ARE A BREEZE

A WALK THROUGH Point Breeze, the neighborhood that formed me and still grips me, stirs memories with every step. It's much quieter now, unlike the Baby Boom era with its scores of large families. In those days the shouts of children were incessant, playing wiffle ball, Release, Kick the Can, or just running about looking for fun or trouble. It's a small patch, barely more than a half mile in any direction, yet its history and celebrity surpass much larger areas.

First, the history: Judge William Wilkins, U.S. Senator and Ambassador to Russia under President Andrew Jackson, built his mansion in 1836 on his estate that covered most of what is now Point Breeze. As Pittsburgh became an industrial powerhouse, many of the wealthy built mansions on Penn Avenue, which became known as "Millionaires Row." Internationally known tycoons H.J. Heinz, Henry Clay Frick, Andrew and Thomas Carnegie, Thomas Mellon, and George Westinghouse lived there. Other lesser known aristocrats lived nearby, escaping the smoke and grit of the factories along the rivers. At around the time the nineteenth century turned into the twentieth, residents of Pittsburgh's East End possessed about 40% of the world's wealth, most of them living in what is now Point Breeze. A residential neighborhood of both upscale and modest homes grew around the mansions, and still thrives today.

The "Breeze," as it's been known since the 1960's, has spawned a list of notables that is remarkable, almost unbelievable, for its size. You want a tour of renowned writers' homes? Let's start with the four Pulitzer Prize winners. A five minute walk takes you past the childhood homes of David McCullough (1982, 1993, 2002) Norman Miller (1964) Annie Dillard (1975) and Mary Pat Flaherty (1986, 1995). That's seven Pulitzers. On the way you would pass the childhood homes of award-winning poets Peter Blair, Nancy Kennedy, and Bill Diskin. Other notable writers include novelists Stewart O'Nan, Albert French, Mark Best, and Jesse Andrews, and national political reporter Kathy Kiely. All lived within a few blocks of each other.

In the second half of the twentieth century it was a haven for Steeler brass. Vice President Jack McGinley, his wife Rita Rooney McGinley (sister of Art), publicist Ed Kiely, and business manager Fran Fogarty were residents. A few celebrity athletes made their homes there. Pirate Hall of Famer Willie Stargell, Steeler great L.C Greenwood, and NBA All-Star Connie Hawkins lived there for decades, from their playing days until their deaths.

Pittsburgh Mayor Joseph Barr (1959-1970) made his home there, as did Dick Thornburg, Governor of Pennsylvania (1979-1987) and U.S. Attorney General (1988-1991), along with many judges and state and local elected officials. Current Pittsburgh Mayor Bill Peduto (2014-) lives there now.

Point Breeze, like other Pittsburgh neighborhoods, has no official boundaries. It's all under the city of Pittsburgh government, which is divided into wards. The city has tried to establish neighborhood boundaries on maps, but it's still fuzzy, ultimately the judgment of current and former residents. Traditionally, Catholic parish boundaries were considered indicative. For instance, anyone who attended St. Bede Church or School was considered a "Breezer." A small expansion of city-imposed mythical boundaries (I'm talking one or two blocks) would give us PBS legend Fred Rogers and former Iowa governor Tom Vilsack.

A few more notables: Federated Investors founder John Donahue raised his thirteen children there. KDKA and WPXI newscaster Pat Kiely lived there during her days on the air, and lectored at St. Bede Church. Frank Dileo, who was Michael Jackson's manager and appeared in the movie *Goodfellas*, grew up there, as did jazz musician siblings David and Maureen Budway, and rapper Mac Miller.

The heart and soul of twentieth century Point Breeze was not the celebrities, but the everyday people – the characters – who made it memorable. The neighborhood was considered upscale by outsiders, with many doctors, lawyers, and business owners. But it also included lots of police officers, firefighters, factory workers, and skilled laborers. It had an Irish

Catholic flavor, and that group was the most numerous, but lots of German Catholics, Italian Catholics, Jews, and Protestants lived there.

Most of the Catholic kids went to St. Bede. Protestants, Jews, and some Catholics went to Sterrett or Linden of the Pittsburgh Public Schools system. For high school most went to Central Catholic, Sacred Heart, or Allderdice. A few higher income kids attended Mount Mercy or Shadyside Academy. All of the schools were known for academic excellence.

As I walk, I think of the many nicknames. I mean real nicknames, not temporary or derogatory ones, but ones by which a person was normally called, with only family members and close friends knowing the real names. Besides common ones like Butch, Skip, or Buddy, or ones based on a surname like Fitz, Pik, Huffy, or Wags, there were Skinny and Pudgy, Beans and Tubby, Duke, Tank, Hot Dog, Bunky, Jocko, Jiggs, Tubs, Duck, Kiffer, Crusher, Chickie, Donk, and Bammer. Some of the girls also had colorful nicknames, like Bunchie, Muggsy, Howdy, Mimi, Trinkle, and Footsie. (Do kids have nicknames like that today?)

Point Breeze produced an impressive number of athletes of its own, especially in football, baseball, and girls' softball. Many prominent players at Central Catholic, Allderdice, and Sacred Heart came from a few adjacent blocks in the Breeze. From 1967 to 1975 four starting quarterbacks at Central and two at Allderdice came from those same few blocks. Three outstanding running backs played at Division One college programs, and scores of other football players from the 1960s and 1970s started for high school teams, many some receiving college scholarships and All-America mentions. Most went to top academic universities. Point Breeze spawned several prominent longtime high school coaches, and one NFL coach, Danny Smith, currently with the Steelers. Opportunities for girls were sparse in those days, but some of the quality female softball and basketball players of that era would receive college scholarships today. They earned the respect of their male counterparts on the fields and playgrounds.

From Millionaires Row I pass Clayton, the home of Henry Clay Frick, now part of Frick Museum and Historical Center. When I was a kid, his daughter, Helen Clay Frick, lived there. We called her "Miss Frick." Next to Clayton, where the museums and parking lot are now, was a beautiful grass field we called "the Greens." We played football and baseball games there with up to 25 or 30 kids, sometimes interrupted by Miss Frick's landscapers chasing us away. Across Reynolds Street begins massive and multi-faceted Frick Park, with its Lawn Bowling greens, Waterhouse, woods, athletic fields, playgrounds, and nature center extending well into Squirrel Hill and Regent Square. As kids we explored in the woods, often swinging out over a 40 to 50 foot drop on "Tarzan vines," an extremely dangerous practice that seemed routine at the time. We ventured down to Nine Mile Creek, which we only knew as "Shit Creek" because of its raw sewage and used condoms.

I pass the Frick Park entrance at the circle of Reynolds and South Homewood, with its quaint arched stone walls and shingled roof. A friend and I once blew off a few shingles with a cherry bomb. A few steps and I'm at Homewood Cemetery's Homewood Gate. Just inside are steep hills that provided great sled riding. Venturing farther into the "cemmey" could bring an adrenalin rush from being chased by Frank, the cemetery cop. Crossing the street brings me to Sterrett School. Its dirt field was saturated with black oil in the spring to keep the dust from blowing. We played pickup baseball there in the summer with full teams, nine on a side and latecomers waiting to get in. In the late summer and fall, St. Bede football practiced there. The ground was hard, almost like being tackled in the street, except that you got dirt and grease all over you. We threw the bigger pieces of broken glass to the sidelines before playing. Legend has it that Bill Mazeroski's home run ball from the 1960 World Series, caught by Point Breeze native Andy Jerpe, was lost in the tall weeds at the edge of Sterrett Field.

Like most Pittsburgh neighborhoods, Point Breeze is hilly. Three more blocks brings me to 527 South Murtland, the house where I grew up. Eleven of us lived there in three bedrooms and an attic. We had a garage and basketball court in the back, now a patio. How could it be so quiet? The noise never stopped back then. It was the center of neighborhood activity, with my mother a smiling, welcoming host. The fecundity of the Point

Breeze mothers of the Baby Boom era was staggering, unimaginable by today's standards. Large families were common in many places, but more so in the Breeze. Three or four kids – a large family now – was small then. I can recall sixteen families with nine or more children, and even more in the five to eight range, all within the same small area. I am not exaggerating.

For many years my father was a fixture on our porch, smoking his cigar and accepting waves and honks from pedestrians and cars passing by. He was a gatekeeper to the neighborhood, watching who came and went. Speeders heard a scornful "Hope ya make it Buddy!" from his booming voice. He often drank Iron City beer with his cigar and snacked on Spanish peanuts. If the Pirates were playing he had the radio on, listening to Bob Prince, who was known as "the Gunner." Dad called him "Ocean Mouth." I think I can still smell the cigar smoke and hear the radio.

One more block up Willard Street and I am at St. Bede, where I attended eight years of grade school under the Sisters of St. Joseph, strict but effective teachers. Classes had 50 to 60 students, well-controlled by one nun or lay teacher. I made my first Confession, Holy Communion, and Confirmation there. I was an altar boy, choir boy, and football player. In the 1950s and 1960s many Masses had overflow crowds. The men wore suits, the women wore dresses. On Christmas Eve it was magic, with a life-sized outdoor crèche, luminaria, and the smells of incense, perfume, and flowers. In recent years I have attended a lot of funerals there.

Backtracking past the new St. Bede Activities Center and the old Rectory, I walk up Reynolds Hill, cross Linden, and descend the cobblestone hill to "downtown Point Breeze," a one block section of businesses. The short journey ends at Mellon Park in East Liberty. I played football and baseball there at times, but what I remember most is the sweet aromas from the Nabisco plant. It's now part of Bakery Square.

These fictional stories attempt to capture the flavor of Point Breeze from its earliest times through the twentieth century. I haven't lived there since 1974, but it will always be home. A few of the colorful characters from my youth appear in some form, but all incidents are fictional. You can go home again, but it's never the same.

Paul F. Kennedy
2019

BAPTISM OF DESIRE

"THIS BABY MUST be baptized," said Margaret as she held the swaddled infant girl.

"But we cannot return east; you know we're wanted there," said her husband Peter.

"Then we'll go west."

"West? To the French? Are you daft? There is a state of war between the English and the French. It's too dangerous. Reverend McCain can do it, and we won't have to make a journey."

The idea of Baptism churned in Margaret's head ever since she heard that a Catholic priest resided at the new French fort to the west, Fort Duquesne.

"McCain's a Protestant. I won't have my baby baptized a Protestant."

"It's a Christian Baptism. It will do for now."

"It will not."

Peter deferred to Margaret in matters of religion, since she was so fervent in her beliefs. He was a Catholic too, but on the frontier one had to do what one could. They were on their own, unlike in Baltimore. Despite the harsh frontier life, they found the freedom intoxicating. It didn't matter if you were English, German, or Irish, Catholic or Protestant. You survived by your own wits. They had been indentured servants in Baltimore, but had run away 17 years earlier and headed for the frontier mountains. It had been a hard life but a free one, and Peter valued freedom above all else.

Peter Tobin was born in County Antrim, in Ireland, part of the Ulster plantation. In the 1600's the ruling English drove the Tobins and the other native Irish Catholics off the land and brought in Protestant Scots to farm it. Peter left Ireland as a teenager for Maryland, the only English colony in America that admitted Catholics. He contracted as an" indentured servant." To pay his fare across the Atlantic, he was obligated to work seven years for the Bentons, a wealthy family in Baltimore. While working there he met fellow indentured servant Margaret Gillen of Derry, also a Catholic from Ulster. She worked for a neighboring family. They fell in love, and planned an escape. Peter felt bad about abandoning the Bentons, who had treated him well, but the knowledge that free land was available in the hinterlands of America was too much for him to resist. The looming harsh climate, wild animals, hostile Indians, and hardscrabble existence could not deter him. After what had happened to his ancestors in Ireland, he felt he deserved a chance.

The early years were tough. Clearing land, building a log cabin, and planting crops required constant hard work. But the neighbors (mostly of Ulster Protestant stock) were helpful, game was plentiful, and corn grew well. They survived. Peter became proficient with a rifle, so they always had food.

Peter Tobin was tall and wiry, with dark hair and eyes, and a gaunt, thin face and long nose. His wife Margaret was of average height but strong for her size, with a determination evident in her cute freckly face framed by straight sandy hair.

When the babies started, Margaret had additional burdens, but handled them well. Thomas, James, Rachel, and Peter Junior were all born about two years apart. Michael and Catherine, twins, were born three years after Peter Junior. Her latest, Mary, was a surprise, born five years after the twins. Margaret was nearly 40 and thought it was over, but she saw Mary as a blessing from God.

Despite having no Catholic church or priest in the area, Margaret maintained her Catholic beliefs, celebrating the holidays and saying the rosary. Her first two sons were baptized by a traveling Jesuit missionary. Her other children were not baptized, except for her own "Baptism of Desire" ceremony that she knew didn't really count. That horrible day in 1754 when the Shawnees came, now three years ago, convinced her forever.

The frontier where the Tobins lived had no permanent Indian residents. Many different tribes used it as hunting grounds, with small groups of young warriors moving through quickly. They rarely bothered the settlers, who kept their rifles handy. The Tobins had seen hunting parties on the move. They eyed each other cautiously, but there had been no trouble. Then in 1754 war broke out between the French and the English, and land in the "New World" was hotly contested. Most Indian tribes sided with the French, who they viewed as less of a threat than the English, because the large English population of the American east coast kept encroaching by settlement into Indian hunting grounds.

One October day in 1754, Peter and his two oldest sons were out hunting. A party of Shawnees came to the Tobin cabin, painted for war. Margaret was home with Rachel, 8, Peter Junior, 6, and the three-year-old twins. Half naked and screaming like red devils from hell, they smashed the skulls of Peter Junior and the twins with clubs. They scooped up Rachel and took her, as she screamed for "Mama." By the time Margaret could get to a rifle, they were gone, leaving three prostrate, bleeding children on the ground. The twins were obviously dead. Peter Junior survived for several days in a coma, but never regained consciousness, and died.

When Peter and the boys returned, they flew into a rage, rounding up neighbors to pursue the Shawnees. They found no trace of them. Rachel, they learned, would likely be "adopted into the tribe." The Shawnees and other tribes valued children around Rachel's age – especially girls – as captives.

Margaret was numb with grief for weeks, crying over her dead children, who were buried in little graves by the cabin. She worried most about Rachel; the uncertainty was maddening. When told that Rachel would most likely be kept alive and raised as a Shawnee, she felt her dead children were lucky in comparison.

Mary, her new baby, born two years after the Shawnee raid, was almost a year old. Margaret, with her bone-deep Catholicism, felt that the fates of her children were related to the sacrament of Baptism. Thomas and John had been baptized, and they were healthy. The rest had not been, and had suffered the consequences. Mary had to be baptized.

The journey to Fort Duquesne would be fraught with danger, mostly from hostile Indians, who would regard the Tobins as "English." How ironic! After generations of persecution in Ireland by the English, they were now fair game because they were seen as "English."

They left on borrowed horses and a wagon, killing game for food as they went. On the fourth day they saw a party of Delawares, and made sure their rifles were evident. The Indians didn't bother them. Two days later they came to a wide river, the Monongahela, which led to Fort Duquesne. They followed near the north shore of the river. The terrain was a challenge, but they persisted.

As they approached the confluence of the Monongahela and "La Belle Riviere" (as the Allegheny and Ohio were known at that time) they saw blue-coated French soldiers.

"Arretez! Arretez!" yelled one of them, who seemed to be the leader. Unable to understand French, Peter called out "Hello!"

"Halt!" said the French soldier. The Tobins halted. The soldiers surrounded them with weapons pointed at them.

"Do you speak English?" Peter asked.

"Anglais! Anglais!" shouted the soldiers.

The Tobins set their rifles on the ground. Despite being shorter than the tall Tobin men, the soldiers looked formidable with their crisp uniforms and bayoneted muskets.

"We are not English," Peter announced. "We are Irish – from Ireland."

"Irlandais?" said the leader. *"Irlandais est Anglais."*

Peter tried to communicate. "No – not On – glay. Eer – lon – day… Catholics."

"Catholique?"

"Yes, Catholic. We want Baptism for this baby. We want to see the priest."

"Bapteme… pour l'enfant," said the leader to the others. He spoke to one, who walked off toward the fort.

"Attendez ici!" he shouted to the Tobins. (Wait here.)

After about an hour's wait, the soldier returned with a tall, slim officer, a man with a trim moustache and an air of sophistication about him. The soldiers showed great deference to him.

"I am Lieutenant Jean Dupuis," he told the Tobins. "I speak English."

"Thank you, Sir," said Peter. "We want Baptism for our baby girl. We heard that there is a priest at the fort."

"Are you aware that a state of war exists between England and France?"

"Yes, but we are not English. We are Irish Catholics. We do not take any side in this war."

"Ah, the Irish. Many brave soldiers from there – on both sides of the fight. But to these French you are English."

Dupuis looked the Tobins over, and peered into the face of little Mary. He stroked his moustache and pondered. "You will have your Baptism. Father Baron will perform the ceremony. My men will take your rifles, which will be returned to you when you leave. Follow me."

They saw the small wooden fort near the river forks, with bastions at each corner. Armed blue-coated soldiers abounded. A village of tents surrounded the wooden walls, amid vegetable patches and roaming pigs and chickens. The soldiers and civilian farmers stopped what they were doing and stared at the strange band of "English" settlers with Lieutenant Dupuis. Dupuis shouted commands, and the gates opened.

Inside the fort, the French guards eyed them suspiciously, but with Dupuis leading their little party, no one accosted them. He took them to a small chapel within the fort. It had an altar and several pews. A crucifix hung from the wall behind the altar. A baptismal font stood to the right of the entrance. To the left was a statue of the Blessed Mother.

"Wait here," Dupuis told them. "I will get Father Baron."

Peter and Margaret knelt before the altar and made the sign of the cross. Thomas and James, unsure of what to do, sat in a pew. Nearly two hours later Father Baron arrived, wearing a black cassock and white alb. A husky, red-haired, middle-aged woman accompanied him. Baron was small and slim, with a severe, serious look on his face. He addressed them. *"Bonjour! Je suis Père Denys Baron. Je vais baptizer l'enfant pour vous. Sarah sera la marraine. Un de les freres sera la parraine".*

"I'll be the Godmother," piped up the red-haired lady, with a familiar accent. "One of your boys can be Godfather."

"Thomas," said Margaret.

"I understand you're Irish," said the red-haired lady. "So am I... County Donegal. I work at the fort here. I help keep these French boys in line. It's nice to meet someone from the Auld Sod. I'm Sarah Foley"

"Pleased to meet you," said Peter. "I'm from Antrim, and Margaret is from Derry."

"Splendid!" said Sarah. "What name do you choose for the baby?"

Father Baron peered at Margaret intently as she said "Mary."

He took the baby and said some prayers in Latin. He handed her to Sarah, who held her over the font. Then, pouring water over the baby's head, he said, *"Je vous baptize Marie. IN NOMINI PATRI ET FILII ET SPRITUI SANCTI... AMEN."*

He presented the baby to Margaret and said *"Marie... une enfant de Christ."*

Margaret kissed the baby fondly, and smiled. Peter thought it was the first time she had smiled since the day of the Shawnees. Peter kissed the baby and said, "Bless you, little Mary."

"Marie," Margaret corrected him. "Her name is Marie."

Father Baron blessed them and said, *"Bon voyage, Irlandais. Que Dieu vous benisse et vous garde."*

Sarah interpreted for them "Have a good trip, you Irish. May God bless you and keep you safe."

THE FOLLOWING YEAR, 1758, the French burned and abandoned Fort Duquesne as a large British army under General John Forbes approached. Forbes dubbed the site "Pittsborough," and the British commenced building a massive structure they called "Fort Pitt." It was 18 acres, many times the size of Fort Duquesne. The frontier became safer for settlers as the French and their Indian allies retreated west.

Marie Tobin grew to be a healthy little girl. Her brother Thomas, her Godfather, watched over her like a mother red hawk.

In October of 1764 the British under Swiss mercenary Colonel Henri Bouquet led an army of 1500 into Ohio and compelled the weakened Indian tribes to return all white captives. The Indians reluctantly returned 206 captives, most of whom they considered adopted members of their tribes. The Shawnees held out. Bouquet took some of them hostage, and the Shawnees promised to deliver all remaining captives by the spring of 1765.

On May 10, 1765, the Shawnees delivered the remaining 140 captives to Fort Pitt. Peter and Margaret, along with many other white families, waited there, hoping to find their abducted children.

Rachel would now be almost 19 years old. What had become of her? What would she look like? Was she even alive? These thoughts went through the minds of Peter and Margaret as they waited in the council hall of Fort Pitt.

Across the river to the north, now called the Allegheny, Shawnee men put the captives in canoes and rowed them across to Fort Pitt. The captives were dressed in Shawnee garb, buckskin shirts with long pants for males and long skirts for females. Some wore headbands. All wore moccasins. They looked and moved like Indians, the only difference their paler skin and hair color. As they paraded in, some families recognized their lost ones immediately. Peter and Margaret observed tearful, joyous reunions for some, but a curious reluctance by other captives. These others did not want to leave their Shawnee escorts.

For a time they could not see anyone resembling Rachel. They went searching among the remaining captives, until Peter found a small, buckskin-clad woman in a long skirt and headband, clinging to a Shawnee man. She had the face of a young Margaret Gillen, with freckles and long, sandy-colored hair. It was an eerie vision to Peter, like meeting Margaret all over again in Baltimore.

"Rachel!" he yelled to her. She looked away.

"Rachel! My baby!" yelled Margaret.

The Shawnee pushed her forward. She looked shyly at her parents.

"Mot-tah… mot-tah," she said. *"Nee-la Shawano ich-quay."*

Peter embraced her. She pulled away.

"Mot-tah! Mot-tah! Gaween!" she screamed. *"Nee-la Shawano!"*

"Rachel, baby, we'll take you home," said Margaret. "Your father and mother have come for you."

She sat down on the ground, her eyes wide with fear. She mumbled softly, *"Mot-tah, Mama… Nee-la Shawano."*

Peter picked her up and threw her over his shoulder. She was dead weight. She cried hard, with deep, sad sobs. Peter recognized the cry from his little girl. It was definitely Rachel.

They took her home. She did not seem to recognize her brothers. She had never met her sister Marie. Margaret got her out of the Shawnee clothes and put her in a long linen dress. She screamed and fought for her moccasins, so Margaret let her keep them. At first she refused to speak or eat. After two days, she accepted food.

Margaret said to her, "Good, Rachel, you must eat. You are home now, with your family."

Rachel looked pensive, and finally spoke in halting English. "Mama, I am Shawano. I want to return to my people. I am not *lep-poa*…what is your word – happy?"

"It's your word, too. You are Rachel Tobin and you are home now."

"I am a *wee-wa…* wife!" Rachel said to her.

"You are not!" said Margaret, anger rising in her. "You are not a wife to any heathen Indian. You are a Christian Catholic woman."

"I am not a Christian. The black-robed *peres* try to make us *Catholique* – never! I believe in *Wossa Mon-nit-to*, who watches over her children like a *nooch-coom-tha…* what is your word – grandmother? She will watch over me."

Margaret slapped her across the face. Rachel looked at her defiantly. *"Nee-la Shawano!* I am Shawnee!"

Margaret was heartbroken. Peter consoled her, telling her it would take time for Rachel to adjust. Margaret hoped that prayer and the sacrament of Baptism would help her. She must find a priest.

The next morning, they awoke to find Rachel gone. Peter and the boys set out after her on horseback, thinking she couldn't get far. But they never found her. In that way she truly was Shawnee. After a few more days they gave up the search.

Rachel never returned. Attempts to contact the Shawnees through military officials at Fort Pitt were futile.

The Tobins moved to the area near Fort Pitt, to "Pittsburgh" as it was now called. They cleared unoccupied land north of the place the Indians had called "Squirrel Hill," near the Nine Mile Run. Peter prayed for his lost daughter. He prayed for the grandchildren he would never know, for the Tobin progeny that would live in the Shawnee tribe.

Margaret prayed for Rachel's soul, and for God's mercy for her. She erected a tombstone on the new homestead and carved into it:

RACHEL TOBIN

b. June 30 1746

d. May 10 1765

THE END

THE ROSE OF KERRY

BRIDEY MCGUIRE KNEW she was pretty. Her thick, dark brown hair – a gift from her mother – framed her pleasing face in just the right way. She had a nice figure – good shoulders and a slim waist. She could turn a man's head.

She lived on Thomas Street in Homewood, Pittsburgh's most exclusive suburb, as a domestic servant for the Shaw family. George and Elizabeth Shaw had a beautiful eleven room house with two children and three servants. The other servants were Peggy Griffin, Irish like Bridey, and Gretchen Lantzy, a German girl. Mr. Shaw had done well as an executive in Andrew Carnegie's iron and steel empire. Most of the Homewood mansion dwellers were captains of Pittsburgh's thriving industries. Penn Avenue, just two blocks up from Thomas, was called "Millionaires' Row." Some of its residents were quite famous, like H.J. Heinz, Andrew and Richard Mellon, and Thomas Carnegie, Andrew's brother. George Westinghouse, inventor of the air brake, lived only two blocks from the Shaws, at Thomas and Lang. Most of the homes had servant girls, the majority from Ireland or Germany, but a few from places like Scotland or Sweden. Some had black girls, and a few had resident butlers, who were black. It was a great place to work for an Irish immigrant girl like Bridey, far from the smoke and grime of the poorer Pittsburgh neighborhoods near the factories. The air was fresh and clean – like in her native Kerry.

The work was constant. She had to cook and clean, wash and iron clothes, wash dishes, serve food, and empty chamber pots. Mrs. Shaw could be demanding, but Bridey wasn't afraid of work, having grown up in rural Kerry. She was strong and energetic, and the Shaws liked her.

Her Uncle Pat and Auntie Kate had arranged for her to come to America and stay with them until she found a job. Pittsburgh had lots of jobs for men and women. She was grateful to leave Ireland. It was 1877 now – the Famine had been over for a good twenty years – but the people were still beaten down from its effects. Her father and sister had died young, too weak to fight off disease. Her mother wailed about those awful days, with so many children dead. Ireland had nothing but drudgery and hardscrabble subsistence farming. The threat of eviction loomed over everyone. Any young person with ambition left for America or England, with their booming industries and good jobs. America was a great place to Bridey – the people had spirit and a sense of things getting better.

Her relatives lived in Bayardstown, which they called "the Strip," a lively, crowded, mostly Irish enclave near the Allegheny River and its many factories. Sure it was dirty, and smelly – with black smoke shooting up into red skies over the rivers – but that meant work for anyone who wanted it.

TODAY WAS SATURDAY. She would walk to nearby Homewood Station and take the train into the Strip. She and the other girls rotated weekends off, so someone always covered the work. The trains were a wonderful thing about Pittsburgh. The wealthier people could now easily work Downtown and live in Homewood or East Liberty, away from the city grime. And people like Bridey could travel around the city quickly.

She was to attend a St. Patrick's Day dance that night with Seamus Cronin, who owned a saloon with his brother in the Strip. Uncle Pat had arranged for her to meet Seamus, a man of some means and good prospects. He was much older – 35 to Bridey's 19 – but a man of good reputation. Upon meeting Bridey, he was taken with her beauty, and eager to court her. She wasn't so sure about him, but she agreed to go. She knew he was a good man.

Bridey noticed how men looked at her. Young, handsome men smiled and looked at her longer than was polite. Seamus was a good man, but didn't thrill her. Was it wrong to wish for a "thrilling" man? She didn't ever *have* to marry. She could stay at her servant job forever, and the Shaws would be happy to have her. She could live in their nice house in Homewood, rather than in a hovel in the dirty Strip. Maybe it was better to be paid to cook and clean than to do it for a husband for free. And she could still send money to her family in Ireland, who sorely needed it. But she thought it would be nice to have children someday – sturdy Irish

Americans, raised in Pittsburgh. And Seamus was a good man. Everyone said so.

Uncle Pat met her at the Lawrenceville Station at 33rd Street and Liberty Avenue, about a five block walk from his home. He didn't like for her to walk alone, although she didn't feel there was any danger.

"What a fine girl! The Rose of Kerry!" he greeted her.

"Ah, Uncle Pat!" she responded.

Pat McGuire worked on the railroad. Although in his fifties, he was strong and agile, if a little slower. He was of average height with a scruffy, graying beard and a reddish face. He was cheerful as always, but Bridey thought he looked tired. The Strip was a noisy, bustling place, full of railroad tracks and yards with freight cars screeching and grinding, and smells of smoke and oil. The factories – iron, cork, glass – spewed smoke into the air, creating a dark pall with dirty cinder track roads. It was impossible to keep anything clean. The crowded little houses of the working poor filled in any leftover space, along with packed tenement buildings of single men there to work, sleep and drink.

To Bridey Uncle Pat epitomized the railroad. He had spent his life there. They walked past the big Union Depot building at 33rd Street. At 28th and Liberty they saw freight cars being serviced at the Roundhouse. As they walked toward Mulberry, they passed by street vendors with vegetables, meat, tobacco, and various other goods. They heard music from several basement saloons. There were lots of shoppers and many children shouting, urchins with dirty faces in their little caps and coats. Being from Homewood, Bridey noticed the dark, dusty air right away, but it didn't seem to dampen the spirit of the people. The Strip was crowded and poor, but a part of America's ever-growing industrial might.

Auntie Kate and her daughter Mary were waiting at the door. Kate was tall with a narrow face, and a little paunchy in the middle. Her sinewy, rough hands were typical of a poor housewife. Mary was growing up, now 14 and soon to go to work. "Welcome home, Dearie," Auntie Kate greeted her. Mary smiled, impressed with Bridey's dress and bearing. Pat and Kate still spoke with the Irish brogue, although they had been in Pittsburgh for many years. Their three youngest, Johnny, Tommy and Mary, still lived with them and spoke pure Pittsburgh. Bridey had been in America for four years, but still had a strong Kerry brogue. The Pittsburghers found it cute, especially the way she said her "o's" and "i's." She said "shtove" for stove and "shtar" for "store." She referred to the "cark" (cork) factory. Pittsburgh speech was flatter and broader, especially the way they said words like "house," and the peculiar unrounded "o." They said "you'uns" for plural you; Bridey said "ye."

The little house on Mulberry was humble compared to her place at the Shaws'. It had no indoor plumbing, and was always too cold or too hot. But she never complained. She had stayed here when she first came to America. Pat and Kate had shown her warmth and love, more than her poor family in Kerry could. The boys never seemed to be home. They were always working at the cork factory or at a saloon.

Seamus Cronin came to the door promptly at seven. Auntie Kate answered it.

"A fine man yourself!" she greeted him. "Please come in."

"Evenin' Mrs. McGuire," he said, doffing his top hat. He looked nice in a dark vested suit with a white shirt and thin black tie. He was a broad-shouldered, rugged-looking man with dark hair slicked back and a bushy moustache. He had bushy eyebrows above serious hazel eyes. He looked at Bridey, sitting with Pat at the kitchen table. She looked beautiful in a long black dress, her comely figure evident. The thick dark hair gave her a stark look around the pretty face and radiant green eyes.

"Evenin' Mr. McGuire... and Bridey," said Seamus.

They both stood up. "Hello Seamus," they said in unison. Bridey offered her hand, which he kissed.

"You look beautiful," he said to Bridey, who smiled.

"A real Rose of Kerry," chimed Pat.

"We'll miss ya tonight, Mr. McGuire," said Seamus.

"I need my rest, Seamus. Long hours… and the wage cuts and extra work shifts…"

His voice tailed off. Seamus nodded in sympathy. The railroad workers had been hit with a ten percent cut and layoffs, increasing the work for those remaining.

They said their good-byes and began the short walk to the Hibernian Association Hall on 26th Street. "It should be a grand affair tonight," said Seamus. Some of the boys have already had a few too many, but they'll be OK. Lots of us marched in the parade downtown, y'know. There were bands and war veterans, police, firemen, and the politicians, of course."

She noticed he used the peculiar Pittsburgh "dahntahn."

At the hall the president of the Association, William Bulger, opened with a brief speech about the importance of remembering Ireland and the starving poor, and of keeping strong in the Catholic faith. "We must never forget we're Irish, patriotic Americans, and Catholics faithful to the Holy Father in Rome…" Unable to refrain from the irreverent quip, he added, "…even if he is a Dago."

The traditional ham and cabbage with potatoes and soda bread was served in buffet style, along with mugs of dark strong porter. Bridey took the occasional porter, but wasn't fond of it. Seamus recommended a lighter lager beer, Iron City. "Made right up the street from here in Lawrenceville." It wasn't bad – it went well with the dinner.

The crowd included men of various ages, but mostly younger. Some brought wives or dates; some came alone. They were a rough crowd, men who worked hard in the dirty factories or on the railroad, and liked to let loose when they had the chance. Most would end up drunk or close to it tonight, and stagger into Mass the next morning with a hangover. But they knew how to have fun, and liked to dance.

After dinner the band started playing, lively jigs and reels from Ireland, and the dance floor quickly filled. Bridey could dance well, and she noticed Seamus wasn't too bad either. After a few fast ones, they sat down for a break. She noticed a tall, wiry dark-haired young man dancing with girl after girl. My God he was handsome! His graceful movements added to the aura, along with laughing eyes and an alluring smile. She wanted to ask Seamus who he was, but thought better of it. At one point their eyes met, and her heart melted. She hoped Seamus didn't notice. *Rory* she heard them call him.

A fight between two over-imbibers broke out, but was quickly stopped by two stout security men. They threw the troublemakers out roughly – the "bum's rush." It only amused the crowd, who were used to such shenanigans. Fighting was common among young men in the Strip. It was usually a quick row over some minor offense, followed by the opponents making up and getting further drunk together. But sometimes it got nasty, with eye gouging, ear biting, and bashing each other with objects.

Near the end of the night the Civil War veterans gathered to sing "Battle Cry of Freedom." Seamus had been a Union soldier – he was at Gettysburg and Antietam with the 64th Pennsylvania Regiment – and joined in.

> *Yes we'll rally round the flag, boys*
> *We'll rally round the flag,*
> *Shouting the battle cry of freedom.*

Bridey was getting to like Seamus. He was a good and decent man, like everyone said.

The affair ended with a rendition of "A Nation Once Again," the Irish anthem of hoped-for freedom, sung by all.

> *When boyhood's fire was in my blood,*
> *I read of ancient free men.*
> *For Greece or Rome who bravely stood,*
> *Three hundred men and three men.*
> *And then I prayed I yet might see,*
> *Our fetters rent in twain,*
> *And Ireland long a province be,*
> *A nation once again.*
> *A nation once again,*

A nation once again,
And Ireland long a province be,
A nation once again.

IT WAS LOUD and rousing, and the singers cheered themselves when it ended. Bridey felt exuberant from the music. How tragic that Ireland couldn't be free like the United States. As they left the hall, another fight erupted outside. It sounded like a good one from the cheering.

Seamus walked her home and kissed her nicely at the doorstep. She felt guilty because she wished it was "Rory."

AFTER SUNDAY MASS at St. Patrick's, Bridey had tea and scones with Pat, Kate, and Mary. She gathered her things and prepared to walk to the train station. Tired old Uncle Pat was preparing to walk with her.

"I'll be fine Uncle, ya needn't walk with me. The gang boys and ruffians are all sleepin' it off."

"It is Sunday. I suppose you can manage."

The shops were closed and not many people were on the streets. She saw a tall young man walking toward her in cap and jacket – headed to work? It was him! Rory from the dance! He looked at her and smiled. She felt weak in the stomach.

"The iron works never stop," he announced in a pleasing, resonant voice.

She nodded weakly.

"A good day to you – Bridey!"

His presumption jolted her from her stupor.

"And how d'ya know my name, Mister?"

"A good guess. It's either Mary or Maggie or Katie or Bridie. Irish girls don't get too imaginative in their names."

"Well Bridey it is – but I spell it differently – with an e-y at the end. If ya know how to read."

"I can read – and write and cipher too. Just ask the Sisters of Mercy at St. Patrick's."

"Well good for you." He doffed his cap.

"Rory O'Grady it is… Miss Bridey McGuire."

"And ya know my last name do ya?"

"It's a small Strip, colleen. Now I have to get to work. Have a fine trip home."

He turned and walked off. *Rory O'Grady.* She thought of him the whole way home.

Three weeks later it was Sunday, April 8th, the week after Easter. The servant girls were given time to attend church. Most were Irish and German Catholics. Since it was a crisp, sunny morning, Bridey and several others walked the mile or so to Sacred Heart Church on Centre Avenue in East Liberty. After Mass, they began the walk home.

"Top o' the mornin' ladies," she heard from behind. It was Rory's sweet voice. Bridey turned and answered, "And a fine rest o' the day to you."

He was clean and handsome in a dark suit and top hat, his "Sunday clothes."

"Ya can't get rid of me so easily, Miss Bridey McGuire."

"I wasn't hopin' to."

He smiled. "Ah, music to my ears. Can I walk ya home?"

"You can, indeed." The other girls walked on ahead.

"So, ya work out here in one of the big mansions, I take it."

"I do. The Shaws, on Thomas."

"And how did Mr. Shaw steal his money?"

"Shteal it? He's a vice-president for McClelland Iron Works."

"I'll tell ya where he got his money. Yer lookin' at it. From me and the other workers he pays next to nothing and then pockets a big profit. They always try to keep down our wages and keep out unions. It isn't fair."

"Fair or not, ye still have work."

"You don't understand, Kerry girl. When the Panic hit in seventy-three, they cut our wages. We have to fight for every penny. Now we have the Amalgamated Union, which they despise."

"Who's they?"

"The rich people, like the ones you work for in Homewood. They got their wealth by exploiting the working man."

Bridey pondered his assertions. "All I know is, here there's work. If you want to see poor, go to Ireland."

"But that's how they do it," Rory answered, excited. "They bring in people who don't know any better, who are desperate. Ignorant bog men from places like Kerry, and now the Polish, and others…"

"I BEG YOUR pardon – I'm not ignorant," she interrupted.

"I didn't mean that. It's just the way they operate. No, you're not ignorant a'tall. Not a'tall."

They walked by the Point Breeze Inn at Penn and Fifth, and saw the hacks standing with their horse-drawn carriages. The trains were putting them out of business. They walked by mansions that Bridey pointed out were owned by Mellon, Heinz and Carnegie. Rory explained how each had exploited the poor. As they approached the Shaw house on Thomas, Rory asked, "Can I see you again?"

"Yes, but leave the soapbox behind," she laughed.

"It's what I believe, Bridey. It's the truth."

She gave him a quick kiss. "I'm usually off Sundays. I'll look for you at the Inn."

They held each other's eyes for a moment, and then parted.

THE FOLLOWING SUNDAY Rory was waiting for her at the Point Breeze Inn. He looked quite handsome in his white shirt and tweed coat, a little worn but somehow comely on his well-formed body.

"A fine afternoon, Bridey. Where wouldja like to go?"

She carried a small picnic basket. "There's a fine wee meadow above Penn, on the Wilkins estate. I brought a bit of bread and cheese, and cake. We can make a nice little picnic there."

"All from the table of the great Mr. Shaw, no less."

"The very one – and delicious."

They walked down Penn and made a right onto Homewood Avenue, no more than a dirt road with ditches alongside it. They passed Edgerton, another dirt road, and came upon Bridey's meadow, a clearing within stately oak and maple trees on rolling hills.

"The girls and I found this place, we did. It's owned by Mr. William Coleman, but no one ever bothers us. They call it the Wilkins estate. Judge Wilkins owned it before Mr. Coleman, but he died, and Mr. Coleman bought it."

"And who is this great Mr. Coleman, who lets a Kerry girl grace his property?"

"He's a coal and oil man, a partner of Carnegie. He has the grandest estate around here. It's lovely land – like Kerry."

Rory looked around and took it all in.

"So Mr. Coleman owns all this land?"

"As far as you can see. Take a deep breath, Shtrip boy, but slowly. The fresh air might shock you."

"What if he and Carnegie and all the other rich men bought everything, and told us poor folks to get off the earth?"

"Why then they'd have no workers to exploit, no way to keep the money rolling in."

Rory laughed. He had no answer for that. He liked the way Bridey could defuse his ranting with her wit.

After eating, they lay on a small blanket. Rory put his arms around her. He embraced her tightly. Bridey looked into his bright blue eyes, and they kissed. She hungered for his full lips and chiseled face. She felt his hair falling over her cheeks, his tongue, his strong body. Her face felt hot. She tingled through her stomach, her loins, her legs. She wanted this moment to never end. Rory was hers. They lay together and held each other for a long time, the sun moving in and out of the clouds as they clutched each other, silent.

He walked her across Penn and over to Lang, turning down toward Thomas.

"George Westinghouse lives there," she pointed out. "The one who owns the air brake factory in the Shtrip. He's an inventor. His girls tell me he's a brilliant man. He's invented many things, not just the air brake."

"He should invent a way to share his profits with his workers."

"Oh shtop!" She slapped him playfully on the shoulder. They stopped in front of the Shaw house, and kissed politely.

"I wouldn't want to dirty the parlor of the great Mr. Shaw," said Rory.

"Rory... so bitter always."

His expression changed – harder – and he spoke slowly.

"My father died in the mill. An accident, they said. Ya know what we got for it? Nothin'. And my mother died from childbirth and my baby sister from the cholera... both too poor to receive any medical care. So don't tell me I'm too bitter."

She put her hands on his cheeks. "Oh, my poor boy... my poor boy."

He softened, and looked at her lovingly again. They stared into each other's eyes, not wanting to part. Rory broke the silence.

"See you next Sunday?"

"I work next Sunday. See you in two weeks."

"Surely."

BRIDEY AND RORY met several more times and walked to the meadow on the Wilkins estate. One hot June Sunday, Rory announced that he had prepared a song for her. He looked into her eyes and sang in a fine baritone.

The pale moon was rising above the green mountain,
The sun was declining beneath the blue sea.
When I strayed with my love to the pure crystal fountain,
That stands in the beautiful Vale of Tralee.

She was lovely and fair as the rose of the summer,
Yet 'twas not her beauty alone that won me.
Oh no! "Twas the truth in her eye ever beaming,
That made me love Bridey, the Rose of Tralee.

Bridey was touched, and pulled him to her. He kissed her all over, her lips, eyes, ears, cheeks. He fondled her thick dark hair, kissing it and spreading it over his face. Writhing against each other, they rolled behind a tree. He took her face in his hands.

"I love you Bridey," he gasped, breathing hard. "I want to marry you. We can be… happy together."

Their lips pressed hard, hurting. She grasped his broad shoulders, feeling his upper arm muscles rippling through his shirt. She felt his strong, calloused hands on her hot face and neck, their lips never parting as they pulled closer… closer… lovers uniting in thrilling passion. She wanted all of him. She felt him enter, both rocking in spasms of pure joy. Her whole body tingled, overwhelming her. She had never felt this good. She knew it was wrong, but she didn't care. She wanted Rory more than heaven itself.

Walking her home, Rory told her he would ask Uncle Pat for her hand. Bridey's thoughts raced. What to do about Seamus Cronin? She knew Uncle Pat wanted her to marry him. She must tell him that Rory was her man.

"Oh Rory, I gladly accept. Even if he doesn't agree, I'm shtill yours – always."

"Shtill?"

They laughed and squeezed each other tight.

UNCLE PAT MET her Saturday afternoon at the Lawrenceville station.

"Ah Bridey, ya never looked so beautiful. I have great news. I'll tell ya at the house, with Kate and Mary."

She walked in silence. Poor, tired Uncle Pat. She would have to displease him.

Kate and Mary were waiting at the kitchen table, all smiles. Pat cleared his throat.

"I think ya know what's comin' lass. Seamus Cronin wants to marry ya, a fine man himself."

Bridey was silent, motionless. How to say it? She didn't want to hurt Uncle Pat, but it was her decision, not his.

"Didja hear me, girl?

"Yes, Uncle, I did," she said firmly. She looked down, took a deep breath, and looked up. "And I can't do it. I'm in love with Rory O'Grady and it's him I intend to marry."

Uncle Pat's head flew back. "What? Who's Rory O'Grady?" He rubbed his whiskers, pacing. "Ya mean that hell raiser from Smallman Street – from the tenements? He's just a common laborer, Bridey. He'll never even make puddler or roller. Ye'd marry him over a man with means and decency of Seamus Cronin?"

She spoke softly. "I would. I'm in love with Rory."

"In love? Ya don't know what yer sayin' lass! That *amadan!*"

She looked him in the eye, defiant. "I know what I'm sayin'. And I know what I'm doin'. And you can't shtop me. It's… it's a free country!"

"I won't have it! So you've been sneakin' around? You get that Rory O'Grady out of your mind!"

"I won't! I can't!" she screamed. "And he's no *amadan!*"

"Then go! And come back when you've come to your senses!"

She stormed out of the house, not saying good-bye, and nearly ran the half mile to the train station. On the ride to Homewood she felt pangs of guilt. Uncle Pat had been so good to her, had taken her in, had helped her get her job. But he didn't know love. He had no right to keep her from Rory. She put her hands to her face and sobbed.

In the ensuing weeks Bridey became alarmed – she missed another period. She had never been reliably regular, but it had never been this long. She knew in her heart what it meant. The Shaws would never let her stay and work there with a child. Lots of servant girls she knew had been dismissed for pregnancy. And she knew she would never let her baby be raised by others. She must tell Rory and they must marry quickly. *And to hell with Uncle Pat.*

ON JUNE 10TH the Pennsylvania Railroad, Pat McGuire's employer, cut wages 10% for the second time that year. On Thursday morning, July 19th, the company ordered that all trains run as "doubleheaders," two engines and two trains run by one crew, doubling the work for men who had just had their wages severely cut. The workers went on strike, taking over the trains and stopping all movement on the tracks. Over 1500 freight cars stood idle in Pittsburgh. A Pittsburgh militia force was sent to the Strip, but refused to use force to disperse the strikers, many of whom were their neighbors, friends, and relatives. On Friday, July 20th the state sent 1000 militia from Philadelphia. They arrived the next day, Saturday afternoon. The strikers still defied them, refusing to relinquish railroad property. When the militia began dispersing them with bayonets, some strikers threw stones at them. The militia responded with gunfire, quickly killing twenty and wounding scores more.

At that time most Pittsburgh factories closed Saturday at noon, and remained closed on Sunday. As news of the killings spread, thousands of workers from all over the city swarmed into the Strip. They broke into a gun factory and stole 200 rifles. The militia, faced with overwhelming odds, retreated into the Roundhouse at 28th and Liberty. At its peak the mob comprised 20,000 angry men. They attempted to burn the Roundhouse by running a flaming oil tanker into it. By Sunday dawn the smoke forced the militia to exit, resulting in a gun battle with twenty more killed, including three militia. Both sides suffered many wounded. The area became a sea of blood with dead and wounded bodies strewn across the road and pavement. The militia was forced across the Allegheny River to Sharpsburg, and took refuge in a county workhouse.

The fury of the strikers continued unabated. On Sunday they burned the Union Depot building, railroad offices, freight cars, locomotives, passenger cars, and a hotel. The flames stretched from 33rd Street to the railroad station at 14th Street. Mobs looted the freight cars, offices, buildings, and stores.

BRIDEY AND HER friends walked to Sunday Mass on July 22nd at Sacred Heart. The trains weren't running because the railroad workers had gone on strike. She worried about Uncle Pat. She hadn't spoken to him since their argument over Rory. Now he had lost his income, at least for a while. At Mass Father Ferris asked everyone to pray for the victims of the violence in the railroad strike. Bridey worried. *What violence? God save Uncle Pat!* She knew he was not a rash man, but a peacemaker by nature. Surely he wasn't involved. She overheard a woman say,

"The whole Strip is in flames! Hundreds shot by militia!"

Bridey rushed to her. "Jesus, Mary and Joseph! What have you heard?"

"There's an insurrection. The workers are rioting, burning everything. The soldiers are shooting them down!"

The woman's companions nodded in agreement. A bunch of old biddies spreading rumors, Bridey thought. But her heart beat fast with worry. She hurried home. Mrs. Shaw greeted her with concern in her eyes.

"There's big trouble in the Strip. The workers are setting fires. Militia have been called in and there have been shootings."

Bridey panicked. "God help us and save us! My Uncle Pat is there! I must go!"

"You can't, my dear. The trains aren't running. And it's too dangerous." Mrs. Shaw put her hand on Bridey's shoulder. "You must stay here. Stay here and pray. It will end."

"Shtay? Shtay here with me blood in the midst of a riot? And maybe dead? I won't shtay. I'll run there if I have to."

She noticed Mr. Shaw sitting in his chair in the living room. She knew how he felt about strikes, unions, and the like. He would be angry. He didn't make eye contact with her.

She changed into her work clothes and bolted out the door.

"Bridey! Stop!" yelled Mr. Shaw. She stopped and turned. "I'm sorry, Mr. Shaw. I must go…" she stammered, her voice breaking. She ran on. She had never disobeyed him before.

Bridey knew she couldn't run all the way to the Strip. She had brought money with her to pay a hack. She might find one at Point Breeze Inn. She ran across Thomas and up Dallas, and saw a man sitting idle with his horse and buggy.

"I must go to the Shtrip," she told him, panting.

"Lady, you can't go there. It's a war zone. And I'm not going near there."

"I live there!" she screamed at him. "Just take me close, down Penn to the Arsenal." She showed him her money.

"OK, Arsenal's as far as I go. You're on your own from there. But if you ask me, I'd say stay here until it settles down (dahn)."

"I'm not asking you!"

She climbed in, and they took off. The smell of horse manure reminded her of Kerry. Her heart was beating so fast she thought it would give out, pumping through her neck and temples. She could see smoke from the Strip as they neared the Arsenal at 40th Street. She would walk the rest of the way.

"God Bless you!" she told the hack.

"Lady, you're gonna need it more than me."

She ran seven blocks down Penn Avenue to 33rd Street, and saw the burnt-out Union Depot building. She stopped to catch her breath. She could hear commotion. Crying? Moaning? *God save Uncle Pat!* She walked quickly to 28th, too tired to run now. She could not believe what she saw. Burnt-out railroad cars and buildings… the smoke thick and black, even for the Strip. To her left she could see men lying in the streets, with women bending over them. She saw a priest in black cassock, hearing confessions and giving last rites. She hurried to Mulberry, to home, hoping to find Uncle Pat there alive.

People milled around on Mulberry Street, looking dazed and hot. She burst through the door, to see Uncle Pat on a makeshift table, a bloodstained cloth wrapped around his head. Mary hugged her and started to cry.

"Oh Bridey, it was terrible… so many dead."

Bridey went to her Uncle, whose eyes were closed. She noticed caked blood on the ears, and in his shaggy beard.

"He'll live…" Auntie Kate said. "But he took a helluva beatin' from them bastards… killin' people for tryin' to make a decent living."

Bridey touched his face. His eyes opened.

"Ah, Bridey, you've come home."

"Oh, Uncle, I'm sorry for everything I've said. You've been so good to me. A better father than my own."

Pat spoke weakly, "I'm sorry, too, lass, for what I said about your Rory. He was a brave lad…" Pat's voice tailed off.

"What do you mean… was?" Bridey's heart beat fast again.

Kate put her hand on Bridey's shoulder. "Oh dear, you didn't know. Rory was killed by the soldiers – shot while trying to save a wounded man. He's a hero."

"NO! NO! HE'S NOT A HERO!" she screamed. "HE'S MY RORY! He's to be my husband."

"Oh, Dearie," said Kate. "He's gone… gone to the Lord."

Bridey broke into a savage, otherworldly scream, the keening she had heard at funerals in Kerry. The room fell silent, the others watching as Bridey knelt and keened, tears running down their cheeks. Shaking, she rose and headed for the dying men on 28th Street. Arriving there and hearing the moans, she was numb. She couldn't cry any more.

"RORY!" she yelled to the women. "Have ye seen Rory O'Grady?"

One woman approached her. "He's among the dead," she said bluntly. "Are you Bridey?"

She clutched at the woman's arm. "I am Bridey… I am."

"He said your name as he died. And he sang a song, how curious… The Rose of Tralee. A fine voice he had."

She grabbed the woman's arm. "I must see him."

"Don't… he's gone," said the woman.

Bridey glared, and the woman led her to a makeshift morgue, a tattered tent. The young men were lying in rows, blood running all over the ground. She recognized Rory's corpse by his hat, curiously stuck on his head by matted blood. His eyes were closed; he seemed to be smiling.

"May God have mercy on yer soul," she whispered, kneeling. She sobbed quietly. The woman put her hand on Bridey's shoulder , weeping with her.

Bridey would stay the night at Pat and Kate's. She hated to put the boys out – they would have to sleep on the floor. She knew her days at the Shaw house were numbered. She would miss its spacious rooms, fine furnishings, and cleanliness. But what to do? A baby was growing inside her – Rory's baby. She had known girls fired for becoming pregnant. If unmarried, they could put the child in an orphanage, or keep it. Either way, it was a difficult struggle, a social stigma, and some even rejected by their own families.

That night Kate commanded, "Johnny! Go down to the saloon for whiskey for your father. Perhaps Seamus can spare a bit for a friend."

Seamus! Bridey hadn't seen him in months. "I'll go," she said. "I can pay for it (far it)"

Johnny piped up, "A woman can't go into a saloon."

"I'm paying far the whiskey and I'll fetch it," Bridey told him.

Johnny looked at her like she was crazy, but backed off. He was old enough to know better than to argue with a determined Irish woman, especially his cousin Bridey. She looked around the little house. *Not even a mirror in this Godforsaken hut.*

Bridey walked into the smoky saloon, crowded with dirty, sweating men. Bluish, whitish cigar smoke burned her eyes and nose. She heard shouts. Everyone was angry. Heads turned as they noticed her. A few men whistled. "NO LADIES!" yelled one. "A fine lass – maybe she'll dance for us," said another.

"SHUT UP!" boomed the voice of Seamus Cronin, who took Bridey by the arm into the back room.

"I need whiskey far Uncle Pat," she told him. "I can pay."

Seamus was pensive, slow to respond.

"I won't take your money," he said. "Let me pour you a bit of the stuff."

Their eyes met. Despite her rejection of him, to Seamus she was still the most beautiful woman he had ever seen, the Rose of Kerry, as her uncle called her.

"I'm sorry for your loss," he said. "Rory was a brave lad. I saw many like him in the war, most of them dead on the battlefield." He gave her the whiskey and hesitated. Looking into her eyes, he spoke. "Bridey, after a decent period of mourning, I'd like to pick up where we left off."

Seamus! My salvation! But she couldn't deceive this good man, no matter the consequences.

"You don't want me, Seamus." She looked down. "I have sinned. I have sinned with Rory and am paying the price." A tear ran down her cheek.

Seamus put his big arms around her and pulled her head to his chest. She felt comforted. He held her for a long time, and then spoke. "I'll raise the child as my own. You'll be safe here with me."

Bridey began to cry softly, and hugged him back tightly. Rory was her true love, but he was gone. She would always have him in the little child that grew in her womb, but she would make a life with Seamus. He was a good man. Everyone said so.

THE END

MARTIN'S GIFT

"MAIRTIN, TAKE THE tea now please."

Martin Joyce, dutiful son, served his ailing mother without complaint. She was born in County Galway, in Connemara, and still had the thick brogue of that region. At times she slipped into Irish Gaelic, her first language. Martin knew a few words and phrases, notably *amadan* (fool) and *pog mo thoin*, pronounced "pog-ma-hone," and meaning "kiss my ass." That was a favorite of his deceased father. His mother dozed off, her breathing audible and labored. He heard her mumble "Ach, the *praties* are black. We're going to starve."

He said to her, "We're in Pittsburgh, Mom. You can get all the potatoes you want."

Martin's right knuckles and wrist were a little sore, a hazard of his job as a Pittsburgh city policeman. The previous night he broke up a speakeasy brawl in the Strip. Some crazed Irishman just wouldn't stop, after Martin had calmed everyone else, so Martin had to knock him out. The stubborn Mick had a hard head, but he collapsed after the punch. Martin rarely had to use his night stick.

Martin looked like a block of wood, with his big head, square jaw, and large body. Despite the appearance, he was quite agile and fit. He had reddish brown hair, blue eyes and a pinkish complexion. His face was non-descript, neither handsome nor homely. He could blend into a crowd, and people tended to underestimate him. He had been a solid tackle for the Westinghouse High School football team, and could hold his own with the best street fighters in his neighborhood. It frustrated him that he never got the credit he deserved for his physical abilities. In his mind it was because he wasn't flashy or boastful. His older brother Jack got a football scholarship to Pitt, and went on to dental school. Martin got drafted into the Army and fought in the trenches of the "Great War," not so great to anyone who was there. It was horrible, and he tried to keep it out of his mind.

He was the youngest child of John Patrick and Catherine Flynn Joyce. They had three children, small for an Irish family. Martin's brother Jack, the dentist, had four kids, and his sister Kate had six, more typically

Irish. Martin had seven nieces and three nephews, and his mother was blessed with ten grandchildren.

Martin lived with his mother on Hamilton Avenue in Homewood, in the house where he had grown up. He was devoted to her, as she was to him. People explained his behavior with the adage "An Irishman never marries until his mother dies." If that were so, thought Martin, why did his brother Jack have a wife and four kids? He just did his duty to the woman who had sacrificed everything for him.

As he took her cup and tray to the kitchen, he heard her cough – again. He had seen her deteriorate with some kind of respiratory disease that sapped her strength. Even the doctors weren't sure what it was. At night she liked a glass of "potcheen," Irish moonshine. It helped her sleep. Her once-pretty face was drawn and gaunt, her sharp features accentuated. Her hazel eyes were still bright, but looked worried.

"Ye won't leave me for some pretty colleen now, will ye Mairtin?"

"No, Mom, I'll never leave you, even if I find a pretty colleen. I'll just bring her here to serve you."

She laughed. Martin could make her laugh, and it helped her spirits. The small, frail Catherine had once been a whirlwind of activity, never stopping with the cooking. cleaning, and laundry. She even took in other people's laundry. She ruled the home with strict love and the support of her policeman husband. The neighbors marveled at how such a small woman could give birth to such large children. Size and strength ran in the family, inherited from John Patrick Joyce. Even Martin's sister Kate could handle herself. One of Martin's favorite memories was when Kate caught an older boy, Jimmy Farrell, picking on him. She gave Farrell a thorough thrashing, as Martin watched in delight. Farrell never bothered him again. Martin and Jack were both football lineman, whose wiry little mother didn't even come up to their shoulders.

After the war, Martin became a cop, like his dad. He felt he was too old for college at that point, and didn't have the money for tuition. The police were hiring, and looking for military veterans. He signed up and had a secure job. He was stationed in the Strip, a once mostly Irish neighborhood near downtown Pittsburgh that now had substantial Polish and Italian populations.

When Prohibition came in 1919, the job got more dangerous, with bootlegger gangs fighting each other for the lucrative trade in booze, and forcing tribute from business owners. The taverns became "speakeasies," operating illegally and paying off the police and gangs. Martin often entered them to drink whiskey or beer. Ironically, drinking alcohol was not illegal, just selling or transporting it. They offered free drinks to cops, but Martin insisted on paying. He never accepted bribes, as so many other cops did.

The gangs were mostly Irish or Italian, with a few Jewish ones operating in the Hill District. Gangs usually extorted their own kind, avoiding inter-ethnic turf wars. But it kept the city on edge. As long as Irish killed Irish and Italian killed Italian, it was somewhat acceptable. Pittsburgh had managed to avoid the Irish versus Italian fighting that had erupted in New York and Chicago, leaving the streets strewn with corpses. Fortunately Pittsburgh had no crazy Al Capone trying to take over everything, killing whoever got in his way. Capone was now in federal prison, thank God.

The Strip was run by Pickles O'Rourke, head of a ruthless gang that distributed alcohol and extorted money from honest business owners. Martin knew Pickles, a heel he had pinched for petty theft many times. He got the moniker "Pickles" because as a child he constantly stole pickles out the brine barrel and ran. The hot-tempered little bastard had no respect for anything, even for the cop who had given him a few good whacks. Now he and his henchmen were wealthy beyond their wildest dreams from running booze. This Prohibition had to end. It rewarded the worst elements. Rumor had it ending if Roosevelt was elected the following year.

Pittsburgh's "Strip District" was a bustling amalgamation of railroads, factories, and produce yards along the Allegheny River near downtown Pittsburgh. Once called *La Belle Riviere* (the beautiful river) by the French, it was now a depository of industrial waste, veiled in smoke and dust. Vegetables, baked goods, seafood, and meats were sold on the streets and in shops, mostly to grocers and restaurant owners. Scores of saloons – now "speakeasies" – served the thousands of factory workers and residents. Martin walked a beat there.

The Strip had its sweet side, and not just in the candy stores. Caterina Siragusa worked at Sunseri's Italian store on Penn Avenue. Martin found excuses to visit her there often. She was small and trim, with jet black hair, brown eyes, and olive skin. Martin thought she was quite pretty. Her friendly, easy manner enticed him. They started dating. He took her out to dinner, to parks, and to stage shows. They made an unlikely pair, the large, fair Irishman, and the small dark Italian. It wasn't unheard of for Irish to marry Italian, but it wasn't common. At least she was Catholic. She said that she wasn't Italian, but Sicilian. Martin thought Sicilian was Italian, but she insisted it wasn't. When Martin told his mother about her, she cocked her head, looking puzzled.

"A Dago?" she asked.

"She is Catholic, Mom."

"Of a sort," replied Catherine Joyce.

ONE SATURDAY MARTIN took her to a show at the Nickelodeon in town. Afterward they sat on a bench outside the theater. He put his arm around her.

"I love the feel of your big shoulders, Martin. It makes me feel safe. My big war hero cop."

"The war's not all it's cracked up to be, and I'm no hero. It was horrible."

She patted his hand. "I know. My brother Tony never talks about it. But you can tell me anything you want, or not."

Martin hadn't talked about it either, not even to family or close friends. He spoke slowly.

"It's just… so many nice young guys… killed… or mutilated. I met guys from all over – New York, Texas, California… good guys, all of them. I lost good friends. Some died, some would have been better off dead. And for what?"

His voice tailed off. He shook his head. Caterina cuddled closer.

"But you survived, and so did Tony, thank God."

"Yeah, I survived. Just luck… and my mother's prayers. Sometimes I feel guilty that I made it while so many others didn't. The things I saw…"

Caterina said firmly, "God willed it for you, and for me."

They sat in silence for a long time, Martin's arm around her shoulders. Finally, she changed the subject.

"My parents thought you were nice, but Mama said it's best to stick with your own kind."

"That's what my mom says, too."

"They'll come around. This is America, after all. You weren't fighting for Ireland over there."

"Yeah, and your brother wasn't fighting for Italy."

"Sicily," she corrected him. "It's really a country. Even the language is different. We can talk Sicilian – well, I can't, but my parents can – so that Italians can't understand it. I don't know much of it but there is definitely a difference. The Italian they teach in school over there is not our language."

"I never knew that."

"And I never knew that Irish was a language. I thought all Irish people spoke English."

"In some parts of Ireland, like Galway where my parents came from, they speak Irish. They speak English, too – their own version of it."

"But we're Americans, Martin, born and raised in Pittsburgh. And we'll make beautiful children. But one question remains." She looked deep into his eyes. "Will they drink whiskey or wine?"

Martin laughed. "Both."

PICKLES TRIED SEVERAL times to bribe Martin. Martin recalled their last conversation as he saw the gangster strutting on Smallman Street with two of his lackeys.

"Officer Joyce, a fine afternoon to you. You and I should talk."

"I've nothing to say to you, Pickles."

"Then listen. You can be on my payroll and still collect your shitty copper salary. Lots of your brothers in blue do it. Then you can marry your Dago doll and have a nice life. Can't do that on a cop salary."

He laughed, that silly high-pitched Pickles laugh. Martin saw his diamond rings, his gold watch, his expensive clothing. What kind of world would reward a punk like that? Pickles had bought a beautiful new home on South Dallas Avenue where he lived with his simpleton wife and bratty kids. Did the neighbors know who he was? O'Rourke's cold gray eyes and toothy smile mocked Martin. He wanted to strangle him right there.

"Shove it up your scrawny ass!" Martin snapped at him.

Pickles laughed again. "Hee Hee Hee Hee! Let me know when you're ready. I have a soft spot for you. We go back a long way. In the meantime, don't count on a promotion. Hee Hee Hee Hee!"

Pickles knew how to irritate Martin, who suspected that his prospects for promotion were hampered by being an honest cop.

The next day Martin saw the headline in the Saturday paper:

BOOTLEGGER FRANCIS KILLIAN SLAIN

Lawrenceville bootlegger Francis Killian, leader of a rival gang to O'Rourke's, had been murdered, his bloody body riddled with bullets and left sprawled on the porch of his Point Breeze home on South Murtland Avenue. O'Rourke was the logical suspect, but no one would have the guts to testify against him. Martin heard from the police grapevine that Pickles himself had pulled the trigger. He liked doing his own killing, the sick bastard. But the disturbing part was that there was a witness, a boy of about twelve, who saw the murder and escaped through the yards of the neighborhood. Martin knew Pickles would have the boy killed, just to be safe. That was risky for public opinion, but Martin knew Pickles – murder meant nothing to him. Martin had to find the boy before Pickles did, and protect him.

Martin had to act quickly. He had a nephew about that age who lived in the neighborhood –Kate's son. He went to see them. He told Kate what had happened. She brought Kevin to him at the kitchen table. Martin said,

"Kevin, you know there was a murder yesterday."

"Yes Uncle Martin, they killed Mister Killian."

"They say a boy witnessed it, a boy about your age. Do you know who it was?"

Kevin squirmed in his chair, his eyes darting. His mother commanded, "Kevin, tell your uncle what you know."

The freckle-faced, snubnosed boy, his curly brown hair unruly, set his jaw.

"I don't know nothin'."

Martin looked into Kevin's scared eyes. "Kevin, the boy's life could be in danger. We need to know who it is, so we can protect him."

Kevin reddened, still squirming. His mother yelled at him, "Tell us – or the boy's gonna die!"

Kevin looked like he was going to cry. "I promised not to tell!"

Martin spoke slowly, firmly. "Kevin, tell me now, before it's too late."

"Jerry Campbell," he mumbled, and put his head down on the table.

"Lloyd Street, corner of Edgerton," Kate told him.

Martin walked to the Campbell house, his gun ready. All was calm. He needed to call it in to headquarters. He saw Neil Finnerty, the local beat cop, walking away toward Reynolds Street.

"Neil! Where you going?"

Finnerty walked toward him. "It's OK. The heat's off. There was no witness."

"You knew about Jerry Campbell?"

"Yes, but they just called off the watch. It was a mistake."

Martin knew something wasn't right. O'Rourke controlled so many cops that they left the Campbell house unprotected. O'Rourke's men would be coming. He knew Finnerty was honest.

"Neil, this ain't on the up and up. Just do me a favor. Stay here, watch the place. You know the boy Jimmy – is he in there?"

"Yes."

"Stay here, Neil, unless you want to see him die."

"Sure thing, Martin, sure thing."

Martin knew he had to kill Pickles, and soon. He also knew he would probably die in the effort. But his blood was up – his "Irish" as they called it. His hatred for Pickles overwhelmed him. And something else... the melancholy, the memories of the trenches in France... curdled his dark side, his lust for violence. If Pickles died, and Martin meant to make sure of that, the boy witness wouldn't matter because the killer – Pickles – would be dead. They would let Jerry Campbell live.

Martin hopped a trolley to the Strip, headed for O'Rourke's Smallman Street office. He didn't think Pickles would kill the boy himself – too risky. He would send flunkies to do that. He hoped Pickles was in the office. He knocked on the door, wearing his police uniform and loaded gun. A man answered the door.

"Pickles wants to see me," Martin told him.

"Wait here."

Pickles came to the door. "A fine afternoon to you, Officer Joyce. To what do I owe this kind visit? Come in, please."

Martin entered. There were two armed guards. He had to hit O'Rourke first, and quickly.

"I'm ready to talk. I... I need the money. I'm tired of everyone else but me making dough."

"Hee Hee Hee Hee... I knew you'd come around. I could use a tough copper like you... one who's respected... above suspicion. Come into my office."

Martin feigned nervousness. "Alone, O'Rourke, just you and me."

Pickles nodded to his two armed guards that it was all right. Martin recognized one, Salvatore Gemelli. *So even O'Rourke believes in the melting pot.*

"Leave your gun here," said Gemelli.

A calm came over Martin, the calm that was his gift. In the tensest situations, in war, in football, in a fight, he was perfectly calm, while most men were nervous. *Now*, he thought. *But one last try.*

"I can't," he said. "I'm on duty. It's against the rules." His right hand was ready. *O'Rourke first, then hope for the best.*

"It's OK Sal," said Pickles. "We go way back."

Martin walked into a room with Pickles, who closed the door.

"You're gonna love it, Martin. You'll be rich, just like me. I will pay you double your salary, so I will be your primary source of income. You follow my orders. You report to me weekly, or more often if I say so. Delighted to have you. Did you ever think that the little punk you pinched so many times would become such a prominent citizen of Pittsburgh?"

"No, I didn't. I sure didn't."

Pickles offered his hand, his eyes gleaming.

Martin put his big arms around Pickles and quickly put him in a headlock. He put his gun to the base of his skull. "SAL! MIKE!"Pickles screamed. He tried to bite Martin, who squeezed harder, almost choking the life out of him. The guards rushed in, guns drawn.

"Shoot, and he gets it!" Martin said. *If I get through this, it's God's will. I'll make babies with Caterina.*

"I'll have you… KILLED… FOR THIS!" screamed Pickles, his face red, eyes bulging..

Martin felt good, like the nice buzz from a first shot of potcheen. He was enjoying his gift. He could see the tension and fear in Sal and Mike. They were about to get the shock of their lives.

"Piece-a-shit!" he yelled, and pulled the trigger. BOOM!!! O'Rourke's bloody brains splattered all over the room. When Sal and Mike hesitated for just a split second at the spraying gore, he shot both of them right through the heart. He was surprised at how easy it was. Blood, bits of brain matter, and skull fragments covered the room. The gore was nothing compared to what Martin had seen in the trenches. He put his gun in his holster and walked out, as calmly as if he had just bought a pound of salami from Sunseri's. To his surprise, he had lived – without a scratch on him. He had fully expected to shoot O'Rourke and be gunned down by his henchmen. But O'Rourke had been too trusting. Like so many others, he had underestimated Martin.

Martin's story was that O'Rourke had tried to bribe him, and tried to kill him when he threatened to turn him in. It wasn't the full truth, but not too far off. The important thing to Martin was that Jerry Campbell was safe now. There was no reason to kill him.

The papers ran wild with the story. GANGSTER O'ROURKE KILLED IN POLICE SHOOTOUT screamed the Pittsburgh Post headline. Martin was the hero, an honest cop who had outwitted and outfought three vicious gangsters. Some speculated that he was retaliating for Killian, or that the police had ordered O'Rourke killed. Police insiders knew the story was fishy, but nothing was ever proven to contradict Martin. Officer Finnerty never said a word to Martin, just smiled widely every time he saw him.

MARTIN ASKED CATERINA to marry him, and she accepted. He took her to meet his mother. To his surprise, he was more nervous than he had ever been in his life. His mother was stubborn. He was afraid of what she might say. It didn't go well. Mrs. Joyce was aloof, barely speaking, her lips pursed in resistance. Martin took Caterina home, riding with her on the commuter train which stopped near her home in the Strip. Both were quiet. Caterina was hurt, and Martin was upset with his mother. Caterina finally said, "She doesn't like me."

"She'll come around," Martin answered, patting her hand. "She will."

He knew Caterina would be patient, understanding the ethnic tensions. He saw a tear drop from the corner of her eye, which he could not forget. When Martin returned home, he chastised his mother. "Mom, I am going to marry this girl, and you are going to accept her."

She glared at him, eyes stern. He glared back. Mother and son glared for a full minute, neither flinching. She saw the iron resolve in his big jaw. Catherine knew she was beaten. When her normally easy-going son set his jaw like that, he meant it.

In the second visit, the women got on fine. Caterina was gracious and kind, and Mrs. Joyce recognized that. She also knew her son was watching. Later, she told him, "Mairtin, she's a nice girl. Even if she's a Dago, she's a fine lass, and I'm happy for you."

"Thanks, Mom. Now, we're not going to use that word ever again, understand?"

"I do," she said, sighing. "You won't hear it again."

But she had to have one small token of rebellion. She declared that she would never eat spaghetti. Martin told her she didn't know what she was missing. He thought she'd come around on that, too.

Martin figured that with all the publicity he was safe from retaliation from O'Rourke's gang – or the police – for now. But one could never be sure. If they came for him, he would be ready. And they would underestimate him.

THE END

BLOOD BROTHERS

IT WAS A hot morning in August as I went to get Andy. Joe the milkman drove by, and waved. He often let me ride in his blue and white Harmony Dairy truck. I helped him deliver, and he would give me a free orange drink. But not today. We were going to the cemetery to explore, and to once again foil four-fingered Frank, the cemetery cop.

I picked up Andy at his house on Lloyd Street, and we crossed the street to get Joey. Joey was two years younger, but we let him hang out with us. He was big and tough for his age, and a good athlete.

The three of us had explored "the cemmy" and escaped Frank the Cop many times. We were proud of our perfect record: we had never been caught. Several kids in the neighborhood had been caught by Frank and turned over to juvenile court. That scared everyone else away – all but Andy, Joey, and me. We could outsmart Frank, and outrun him when the time came.

School would be starting in two weeks. Andy and I would be entering sixth grade, and Joey would be entering fourth.

There was much to explore once inside the black iron fence of Homewood Cemetery: woods, the pond, and creeks where we could catch wriggling little salamanders. There was a Chinese section that had both English and Chinese writing on the tombstones, and names like "Woo Bing." There was a Greek section with funny Greek letters and a different kind of cross. There were tombs called "mausoleums" that were almost as big as houses. Some of them had names of rich and famous Pittsburgh families: Frick, Heinz, Benedum, and Mellon. Jock Sutherland's grave was also there. He was an old-time Pitt football coach. We didn't know much about him, but our dads sure thought he was someone special. Speaking of dads, no one ever saw Joey's dad. We heard rumors that he was in prison, but Joey denied it. He just said his dad was "away."

We had three entrance points in the cemetery fence where a bent or missing spire allowed us to enter or exit quickly. Climbing the fence was difficult – without an opening we could never escape Frank. The bent spires were at the top of Willard Street and halfway up Dallas Avenue; the missing spire was at the top of Lang Avenue.

The escape points were strategically placed in the huge cemetery. We didn't create them – there's no way we could have bent or removed those iron spires. But we knew exactly where they were and how far we had to run to get to them from inside the cemetery. Once we were outside of the fence, we were home free. Frank had no authority outside the cemetery.

Once inside, we ambled along the asphalt road to our favorite mausoleum, "The Eye." We could look through the window in the front of it and see inside. It had stone drawers (filled with dead bodies, we assumed) on each wall. On the back wall, facing the front window as we looked through it, was a large stained-glass window. It portrayed a huge eye (the eye of God) looking at his creatures on the earth below. It was a spooky sight, especially with the dead bodies piled in the drawers. One of the drawers had what looked like dried blood dripping down it.

As we moved to the next mausoleum, we heard a stirring in the bushes behind us. Everyone stopped – ready to spring into action. A shy, doe-eyed creature emerged. It was Pete, Joey's little brother.

"Go on home!" yelled Joey.

Pete didn't move.

"Git goin', punk!" said Andy.

We moved on. Pete waited until we were a safe distance ahead, and then followed.

Andy and I were "blood brothers." We had cut our fingers with a knife and let the blood run into each other's cut, making us brothers. Today we were going to do the same to Joey. We took him to a nearby clump of trees.

"Joey, we're gonna make you our blood brother," I said solemnly.

Andy pulled out his pen knife. He made a small cut in Joey's index finger. Big drops of bright red blood rolled down the finger, dripping to the ground. Joey endured it in silence. Then Andy cut his own finger, and pressed to Joey's. We wiped the blood on our shirts. He handed me the knife. I cut my finger, and pressed it to Joey's. We wiped the blood on our shirts. It was done – we were brothers.

We emerged from the trees, three brothers in blood-stained white tee shirts. Boldly, we wandered down to the pond, not far from Frank's office. It was just a matter of time until he saw us. We skimmed stones across the murky pond. Brown-green algae and lime-colored lily pads covered most of its surface. Andy skimmed one all the way across. He was a nice-looking kid with light brown hair and blue eyes, and an easy smile that lit up his face. He was a graceful athlete and fast runner. He had a good arm. Joey had dark wavy hair and a brooding look on his face. His eyebrows were remarkably thick for a young boy. He had dark brown eyes and a pug nose. Despite being two years younger, he was as tall as Andy and me. He was lean and wiry and, like Andy and me, he could run. Andy and I were two of the best athletes in the neighborhood. I was stronger and more powerful; he was quicker and more graceful. But we never competed with each other like we did with other kids. We never fought. We were close friends who always stuck up for each other.

Joey was privileged to be allowed into this close bond, and he knew it. Our acceptance of him gave him enormous prestige, particularly with kids his own age.

Tiring of the pond, we walked back up to the road. A rusty spigot stuck out of the ground. We had used it many times before. We each took a long drink and sloshed water over our sweating faces. It was getting hot.

Pete stood back, watching. Andy threw a stone in his direction. Suddenly a car rounded the bend. We dove behind some nearby tombstones.

"Pete! Get down!" I screamed.

He hit the dirt obediently. It was a blue-and-white Ford Fairlane – not Frank. We rose slowly.

"Get outta here Pete!"

This was serious business – no place for little punks like Pete.

We continued down the road, along the dirt banks, watching for yellow jackets. We threw stones, trying our aim at distant tombstones. We had heard tales of vandalism in the cemetery, but we had never done any of it. Once we knocked over a tombstone by sitting on it, but we didn't mean to. And once we had a flower fight with the flowers on a fresh grave, but we would never desecrate a grave.

"The Buccos ain't gonna do it this year," said Andy.

"No, not like last year," I responded. "It looks like Cincy has it wrapped up."

"Yeah, last year was fun."

"When Maz hit that homer, Man, that was the greatest."

"Yeah… to beat the Yankees – that was somethin'."

"All year we did it. Every game we'd be behind, and then it would come to the eighth inning and we'd come from behind and win it. It was that eighth inning, Man. I remember layin' in bed so many nights waitin' for that eighth inning – and they always came through."

"Yeah, the Pirates ain't nothin' this year."

We were heading for the exit at the top of Lang Avenue. Frank hadn't shown today.

"I heard Frank has a gun," Joey said.

"Oh yeah, it shoots rubber bullets," said Andy. "He shot 'em at me once."

"You ever seen his hand?"

"Yep. His one had has just four fingers and no thumb. It's weird, Man."

Frank's little black car rounded the bend and stopped.

"FRA-A-A-A-A-ANNNK!!!"

We sprinted for the fence. It was maybe a football field away. Andy and I raced evenly, with Joey right behind. Frank, enraged, drove his car up into the grass and headed for the fence, hoping to cut us off from our exit. Then we heard sobs. Pete!

Pete was racing alongside Frank's car, crying, losing ground. Andy, Joey, and I made it to the fence. We slipped through – panting – and turned to watch the drama. Frank pulled his car up to the fence at an angle, trapping Pete between the black iron fence and his shiny black car. He got out. Pete fell to his knees – screaming – his hands trembling.

"JOEY! JOEY!!!" Tears streamed down his reddened face. "AAAAH, HA HA HA!" His terrible screams echoed all the way down Lang Avenue.

Frank approached him, a satisfied gleam in his beady eyes. We backed up slowly, eyes glued on Frank and Pete. Pete, still on his knees, continued to wail. Joey took a step toward the fence.

"Joey! Your perfect record!" yelled Andy.

Joey didn't seem to hear him. He leaped through the fence, back into the cemetery. Tenderly he placed a hand on his hysterical brother's shoulder.

In a flash Frank seized him roughly by the upper arm and shoved him into the back seat of the car. Frank glared at Pete, who scampered into the car behind his brother. Then Frank turned to look at Andy and me.

"Stay outta this Goddamn cemetery, ya riff-raff!"

We watched as the car pulled away with Joey and Pete in the back seat, their arms around each other. Joey was stone-faced, calm. Pete looked scared, his face still red and tearful.

Andy and I walked along the cracked pavement of Lang Avenue, strangely quiet. Andy broke the silence.

"He lost his perfect record."

"I would've done the same thing…" I answered. "That was brave, Man. Joey's brave."

"I hope he don't tell on us."

"He won't. He's tough."

"Yeah, he's pretty tough, but Pete might squeal."

"Nah, Joey won't let him… Joey won't let him."

We headed for Sterrett Field. Maybe it wasn't too late to get into a baseball game."

THE END

BOYCHIKS

IT WAS ANOTHER hot summer day, Pittsburgh muggy, in late August. Kevin figured he'd drop by Billy's house and see what was going on. Little League had ended for the year. Maybe they'd watch St. Bede football practice at Sterrett Field. They were in their two-a-day summer practice.

As he approached Billy's house on Edgerton, he could hear yelling, and whimpers from Billy. Billy came running out, his face wet with tears.

"GET THE HELL OUTTA HERE… YA LOUSE!" his dad screamed.

Billy slowed to a fast walk, Kevin straining to keep up with him.

"He's a jerk… a fuckin' jerk!" Billy stammered, stifling sobs.

Kevin felt bad for him. Billy's dad was mean, and always yelling at him. It wasn't like with most dads – Billy's dad seemed to genuinely not like him. Finally Billy slowed, and calmed down some. "I hate him," he said through gritted teeth. They walked on toward Lloyd Street, not speaking.

Kevin was tall for his age, and slim. He had an impish face, with a few freckles across his nose. He had lots of swirls in the medium brown hair that fell over his forehead. Billy was slightly shorter, with sandy short hair – nearly a crew cut, with a round head and two prominent swirls at the crown. He had a short straight nose and a pained expression. He always looked wary. Both wore the uniform of their age group: blue jeans, white tee shirt, and tennis shoes.

On Lloyd they saw "Johnny Baseball." He always had lots of baseball cards. Johnny was a 30-year-old who loved baseball. He worked in a sheltered workshop for "the handicapped." He had his own spending money, which he used to buy whole boxes of baseball card packs. Kevin and Billy and other kids could only buy one 5-cent pack at a time, begging the money from their parents or helping somebody with a paper route. A pack had five cards and a flat square of pink bubblegum coated with extra sugar. Johnny could buy a hundred or more cards at a time. He always had a stack of several hundred cards with him, and a huge wad of bubblegum in his mouth that puffed out his cheek like a Bill Mazeroski tobacco chaw. Because of the gum, he often had drool dripping from the corners of his mouth.

"Hey, Johnny! Whatcha got?" Kevin shouted. Johnny pulled out a high stack of cards from his big pocket. He wore dark baggy pants and a checked short-sleeve button shirt. He was tall, with a large head, thick black hair, and deep-set eyes. He towered over the boys.

"Just got Walt Dropo, Phil Linz, and Al Kaline," he said in a deep, halting voice. He looked at Billy. "You OK, Billy?"

"Yeah, I'm OK."

Johnny pulled out another card and smiled. "I got Dick Groat."

"WOW! DICK GROAT!" the boys said together. "Let's see it!"

Johnny displayed it proudly. Despite his "handicap" he knew the value of his cards. They knew he wouldn't give up Dick Groat, a star Pirate.

"I'll give you Big Klu for Kaline," Kevin said.

Johnny frowned. "Kaline's batting .320; Klu's average is below .250." Johnny went through his stack one by one as Kevin and Billy checked it.

"Need him… got him… need 'im… need 'im… got 'im…"

They loved to look at Johnny's cards, because he had almost everybody. At least they could see the cards they didn't have.

They started walking toward Jake's Corner Store, when they saw a boxy red huckster truck chugging along. They hollered,

"HEY GIOVANNI!"

"GIOVANNI SPAGHETTI!"

"HEY… GIOOOO – VAAAAAANNEEEE!!!"

The truck stopped suddenly, in the middle of the street. A short elderly man with a full head of wavy gray hair burst from the door, shouting.

"IM-A-GONNA KILL YOU!"

He shook both fists in the air.

"SON OF A BITCH!"

Kevin and Billy ran, laughing at the crazy old man. From a safe distance, Billy stopped, turned, and gave him the finger.

"*BASTARDI!!!*" the old man screamed, and gave chase.

"HOLY SHIT! RUN!"

They sprinted across Edgerton and started down the red brick hill, shoes pounding the pavement, gasping for breath. He was still coming! They ran to the bottom of the hill, near the Frick Park entrance. Giovanni stood at the top of the hill, shaking his fists and shouting.

"That man's crazy," said Kevin. "Whew!"

Billy nodded in agreement.

After exploring the woods in Frick Park for a while, they decided it was safe to come out. They went to Jake's Corner Store to buy some candy and pop.

Jake's store had its own little courtyard, with room for delivery trucks, and metal and wooden crates to sit on. The step up into the store through the slamming door brought one into a world of delights. To the left was a long counter with a cash register and a large menagerie of penny candy. It had forty or fifty different items, all for one cent. A glass jar held full-size pretzel sticks, two cents apiece. The counter included a glass display case of big nickel candy bars like Milky Way, Snickers, Mallo Cup, and Hershey. To the right of the door was a freezer with ice cream, frozen food, and popsicles. Shelves lined all of the walls from top to bottom, stocked with cans and boxes of food. Further down on the right, across from the big counter was a cooler about five feet by three feet, and maybe four feet deep. It had a plethora of pop choices in cold water. Straight back from the front door, toward the rear of the store, was a display case of cheese and cold cuts. Behind that was Gerry the Butcher's room, where he sliced the meat on a blood-stained wooden table.

"KA-PEETZ-NEE-A!" yelled Jake as they walked in. "Ka-peetz-nee-a, mazikim!"

Jake was in his fifties, of average height. He had steel gray hair, curly around the sides, thin on top. He had a huge bulbous nose, both broad and long, with faint veins and tiny craters, that dominated his face. His twinkling eyes and full lips fought for attention around the massive nose.

"Hey! Ka-peetz-nee-a!" Kevin and Billy responded. They had no idea what it meant. Since both were regulars who Jake trusted, they had the run of the store. They went back to watch Gerry slice pieces of meat – whoosh! Fast and efficient, he piled up raw chops. They pulled bottles of pop out of the cooler. Kevin chose his favorite, Tom Tucker grape, while Billy chose 15 ounce Lotta Cola, more pop for the money and good. They used the bottle opener on the cooler. Kevin picked a few pieces of penny candy and a pretzel stick.

"Vat you vant, *putz-lev-a?*" Jake asked.

Kevin set his stuff on the counter, and Jake rung it up on the cash register.

"*Kahk-shee-taa!* Vat you vant?" he said to Billy, who likewise put his stuff on the counter. Jake rung it up.

"Be goot, m*ein boychiks*," he said as they walked out the door.

They sat down on the crates outside, leaning against the stone foundation of the store. Both took a long swig of sweet, cold pop.

"Do you have any idea what he's saying?" Billy asked Kevin.

"No, except 'vat you vant?'" Kevin laughed. My dad says it's Jewish. My mom says it's probably something dirty."

"Yeah. Like kahk-shee-ta. Someone who shits through his cock."

They both laughed, rolling around on the crates, falling to the ground, faces red, stomachs convulsing in the pure ecstasy of unrestrained laughter.

Billy stopped – pensive - the pained expression returning. He spoke quietly. "He... he ain't my real dad. I never told no one that, so don't tell."

Kevin's jaw dropped. "Never, I swear," he said, raising his right arm. "Mother's honor... What do you mean, he's not your real dad?"

The boys looked into each other's eyes, communicating the trust that only true friends had, a sacred bond. Billy said slowly,

"I was born... before Mom married him. I don't even know... who my real dad is."

This was new to Kevin. In the Point Breeze neighborhood almost everybody had a mom and dad, and lots of kids. Even a family with an only child was odd. A few kids had only a mom because their dad had died, but that was rare, and Kevin felt sorry for them. He felt bad for Billy, but he also felt the warmth of friendship, appreciating the confidence Billy had in him. He knew it wasn't easy for Billy to tell him this. They ate and drank without speaking, their silence reinforcing the solemnity of Billy's revelation.

STERRETT FIELD WAS a City of Pittsburgh "oil field." In the Spring, city workers spread black, gooey oil over the entire field. Without the oil, it would be a "dust bowl." No grass ever grew there. The field could not be used for several days until the oil dried, sort of. When completed, the field was hard and black, with little rocks and pebbles. The oil never fully dried. At Allderdice High School, another "oil field" where the boys played some of their Little League games, players scraped their fingers on the ground and dabbed the oil beneath their eyes to make black lines that cut down the sun's glare.

St. Bede's football team practiced at Sterrett, and lots of local people turned out to watch – parents, former players, and younger kids not yet old enough to play. The smell of oil, dirt, and sweat permeated the air, along with cigarette smoke from spectators. Practice uniforms never got completely clean due to the oil stains.

Kevin and Billy watched in fascination. The crack of helmets, the sound of spikes scraping the hard ground, the grunts of the players produced a cacophony pierced by the coaches' whistles, stopping and starting the action. Coach Hogan, powerfully built in a white polo shirt, blue sweat pants, spikes, and a blue baseball cap, supervised the action. It looked hard – not fun like baseball – but it was a way to prove that you had "guts" and were willing to fight for your school against rivals from other neighborhoods. There was talk of starting a "JV" team of fifth and sixth graders, but it hadn't happened yet. Kevin and Billy were a year away from participating, if they chose to do so when the time came.

"Hey! Punk!" Billy heard a familiar voice, one he didn't like. It was smart aleck Jeff, a boy a few years older who picked on him. Jeff was standing with a bunch of friends. He had slicked-back dark hair with a pointed nose and chin that Billy felt made him look like a rat. Billy ignored him.

"Punk! I'm talkin' to you!"

Billy felt a pebble sting his arm. He turned, angered, and muttered "Fuck you!" Jeff came over to him, standing a full head taller. Kevin and Billy started to walk away. Jeff shoved Billy to the ground and stood over him.

"Don't walk away from me - JAGOFF!"

Billy rose, red with rage, and dove into Jeff. Jeff grabbed him by the shoulders, turned him, and shoved him face first into the hard oil field. Billy felt the left side of his face burn, and heard Jeff laughing. Then he heard a whistle pierce the air. He saw Coach Hogan moving toward Jeff. The coach, whistle dangling from his neck, looked like a giant to Billy.

"GET OFF MY FIELD!!!" the coach screamed at Jeff. The whole field went quiet. Jeff sneered. "I don't have to. It ain't your field."

Hogan ran at him. "GET THE HELL OUTTA HERE!!!"

Jeff turned and ran up the steps into the playground, to the sound of snickers and laughter. Embarrassed, he continued to walk away. Hogan walked over to Billy, whose face was a mess of dirt, oil, and brush burn.

"Any time you want to play here, son, you let me know."

Kevin was proud of Billy. He had stood up to an older bully, and even been praised by Coach Hogan. He admired that in Billy. He wouldn't let anyone push him around.

THE NEXT DAY, Billy's mother sent him to Jake's to pick up a few things. Johnny Baseball was in front of him, buying baseball cards.

"Baseball cards, always baseball cards Johnny," proclaimed Jake. Johnny half-smiled, eager to get home and open the packs in his new box of cards.

Billy told Jake he needed a pound of chipped ham, a half gallon of Sealtest van-choc-straw ice cream, and a loaf of Town Talk bread. Jake looked at him. The scrapes on his left cheek were a scabby red.

"Mein boy! Vat happened, boychik?"

"Billy looked down. "Nothin'..."

Jake bent over and whispered in his ear. "That Jeff... he's a trouble-maker. I told him he can't come here no more. If he vas twice as smart he'd be an idiot. He's a real *shtunk*."

Billy perked up. "A... shtunk? What's that?"

Jake's eyes twinkled behind the massive nose. "That's Jeff."

Walking home, Billy passed two nuns, a reminder that school would start soon. They were Sisters of St. Joseph, who taught at St. Bede. They wore the black habits with big starched bib collars, and black-and-white head coverings that revealed only their faces, no hair. Billy had never seen these two before. They were young, and must be new to St. Bede. One was quite pretty. He hoped he'd be in her class.

"Good afternoon, Sisters," he said in the formal way he had been taught to address nuns.

"Good afternoon," they said together, smiling at him.

As he walked along tree-lined Reynolds Street, Billy found himself wishing that his parents could be more like Kevin's. Kevin's mom seemed happy and secure. His dad was strict, but kind, someone to look up to. Billy's mom was afraid of his dad, who wasn't even his "real dad." That worried him. He wanted nothing more than for his mom to be happy. In the distance he saw Giovanni's boxy red truck chugging along, and grinned. *Crazy old man.* He speeded up. He wanted to get home before the ice cream got soft.

THE END

MAGGIE'S HEART

MAGGIE MCENERY WAS angry. She heard the disturbance next door, that Johnny Burrows yelling and screaming at his wife Tracy. They were a nice-looking young couple, Johnny with his slicked-back hair and handsome face, Tracy with her reddish blonde hair and pretty freckled face. But there was something Maggie didn't like about Johnny. He was the kind of guy who was always combing his hair, too much into his own appearance. He had a flashy car, a newer model yellow Impala SS convertible. It was too much car for his income, with the two little ones, a boy and a girl, clinging to Tracy. And he had a perpetual five-o'clock shadow that gave him a sinister look. That bothered Maggie, although she didn't know why. He worked at Mine Safety Appliances at Penn and Braddock, just a few blocks away. He couldn't make much money, but at least he kept a steady job.

Tracy was sweet, but submissive. Johnny bossed her around a bit too much for Maggie's taste. Maggie had noticed some bruises on Tracy's face a few weeks ago, covered with makeup but obvious to the trained eye of Maggie, an emergency room nurse at Pittsburgh Hospital.

Tracy seemed to like Maggie, who was in her late fifties, old enough to be Tracy's mother. The little tots accepted Maggie, allowing her to hold them like a grandma.

Maggie watched Johnny leave the house quickly, looking angry as he peeled out in the yellow Impala. It seemed to Maggie that it was mostly smaller guys who were aggressive and hit women, smaller guys like Johnny. Her own husband Eamon, a hard-working, strong six-footer, was secure in himself and kind to others. Maybe it was the "Napoleonic Complex" thing she had read about, a small man feeling a need to prove himself. Maybe it was just the upbringing. Anyway, she had seen too much of it at the hospital.

She decided to go over and talk to Tracy. Tracy let her in. Maggie could see that she had been crying – no bruises thank God – as she dabbed her tears with a tissue.

"Is everything OK" Maggie asked.

"Oh, yes, of course," Tracy said, trying to force a smile.

"I heard yelling, so I wondered…"

"It's OK, Maggie. He has a temper… but… we do love each other."

"You know, if he would ever lay his hands on you… you shouldn't allow that. You don't have to take that."

"Johnny? Oh, he wouldn't do that… not to me."

The children looked sad, but cheered up when Maggie went to them.

"Little Johnny, Linda, how are my little ones?"

They clung to her, laughing as she bounced them on her knees. Maggie could handle the two easily, big as she was. She had a broad nose and wide jaw on a large head, softened by kind, caring blue eyes. Her hair was ultra-thick and wavy, with a mind of its own, giving her natural "big hair." Formerly a chestnut brown, it was now graying. She had a booming voice with a hint of Irish brogue. With her square shoulders and erect posture, she looked imposing. Her quick, forthright walk was that of an athlete. She had been a standout basketball player at Holy Rosary High School in Homewood in the late 1930's. She and Peg O'Malley were the "Twin Towers." Peg could shoot, and Maggie, with her 5'10" height and large frame, could rebound. They were unstoppable, winning two Catholic Diocesan championships. Those were the days.

She and Eamon, like almost everyone else in Homewood, had moved out by the early 1960's. The neighborhood had gotten bad, with crime and danger rampant. It had been a pleasant mix of Irish, German, Italian, and Black, until the urban renewal projects of the 1950's. The new blacks moving in were "riff-raff," unlike the middle class families she had grown up with. The riots of 1968 – just last year - finished it off.

So many Homewood families moved to Point Breeze that Maggie felt at home there, like it was "Homewood South." Most were Catholic, with so many joining St. Bede that some jokingly called it "Holy Rosary Bedes."

Maggie loved to reminisce about the old days. At her all-girls Catholic high school, basketball was a big sport, and Maggie was good at it. They didn't seem to have much in the way of sports for girls in Point Breeze, although changes were brewing. Basketball made a girl like Maggie feel good about herself. Tall and broad-shouldered, she was "not quite pretty." But on the court she felt at home, and won the respect of girls and boys alike.

As she bounced the tots on her knees, she reflected on what she had seen at Pittsburgh Hospital. She had seen physically abused women; most of them tried to deny it. What galled Maggie was that they accepted it. She didn't want Little Johnny or Linda, bouncing on her knees, to grow up with that, thinking it was normal. She looked at sweet little Tracy. *Goddammit, stand up for yourself,* she thought.

When Eamon came home that night, Maggie told him about her suspicions.

"Maybe you should say something to him about it," she told him. "He respects you."

Everyone respected Eamon, a self-employed painter, a man who worked hard all day, scraping, priming, painting, climbing up on scaffolding. The rough, cracked, reddish skin on his hands and arms looked older than his age. He was always tired when he came home. In his younger days he had the time and energy to coach Little League and help organize church functions. Now business was good – he didn't even need to advertise. He never turned down a job. He remembered when work was scarce and he had kids to raise. He answered Maggie,

"Honey, you don't know for sure what's going on. To interfere might only make things worse. And you know what the cops say. Domestic calls are the worst, the most emotional. They subdue the guy and then the woman takes his side. It's a bad situation."

Maggie clenched her fists. "I do know what's going on, and I've seen what can happen. We have to stop that Johnny Burrows!" *Damn Eamon! Always so wise... so prudent.*

TWO WEEKS LATER she heard more commotion next door. It sounded bad. She had to go. At the front door she heard them both screaming, and what sounded like the "crack" of a punch landing. She burst through the door. "What's going on here?"

She saw Johnny standing over Tracy, who sat on the floor with her back to the wall. Her left eye was swollen shut. She hung her head in shame. The children were cowering in a corner, whimpering, with their arms around each other. Maggie thought her heart would break.

"Get out of here, Maggie!" Johnny yelled. "This is none of your business!"

She felt the anger swelling in her. "You've committed a crime, Johnny Burrows! It's everybody's business!" She couldn't contain herself and moved toward him. "YOU LITTLE SLIME!"

Johnny's face reddened. She could see the fire in his eyes as he approached her.

"GET OUTTA MY HOUSE! YOU BIG APE!"

Maggie went blank, so angry she couldn't think. She saw the women in the emergency room, the broken bones, the blackened eyes, the missing teeth, the tears of despair. She swung with all of her might, her big fist connecting with Johnny's nose, knocking him to the floor.

"OWWWWWWWL..." He held his nose with both hands, blood seeping through his fingers. "I think it's broken," he moaned.

"I hope so," said Maggie.

"I'll file assault charges against you Maggie... you..."

"Oh will you? And tell the cops a woman knocked you on your ass – and one thirty years your senior at that? I don't think so."

She turned to Tracy. "And you – you stand up for yourself! If it happens again, you tell the proper authorities!"

She spun on her heels and walked out the door.

WHEN EAMON CAME home that night, she told him the story. He began to sing, to the tune of "Clancy Lowered the Boom.".

BOOM BOOM BOOM BOOM, BOOM BOOM BOOM BOOM,
Oh that Maggie, Oh that Maggie,

Whenever they got her Irish up,

Maggie lowered the BOOM! BOOM BOOM BOOM…

Maggie laughed awkwardly. "I guess I'm a bad person, turning to violence… no better than Johnny Burrows."

"You did what you had to do in the situation. Maggie, your heart's so big that sometimes you just can't contain it. Poor Johnny Burrows felt the wrath of it… and he deserved it."

Eamon put his arm around her and kissed her, saying, "If it happens again, we'll try a more civil approach… or I'll settle it once and for all. You're feeling guilty, aren't you?"

Her eyes twinkled, unsure. "I am."

"But you'd do it again if you had to, wouldn't you?"

She smiled. "I would."

EAMON MCENERY DIED of a heart attack in 1982, a year after he stopped working. Maggie had lost touch with the Burrows family, who moved away shortly after her confrontation with Johnny. At the funeral home for Eamon's evening visitation she had a surprise visitor. She didn't recognize the small blonde well-dressed woman who patiently waited to talk with her.

"Maggie, I'm Tracy… Henderson… you knew me as Burrows. I'm so sorry about Eamon."

"Oh my goodness! Tracy!" Maggie embraced her. "You moved out to Penn Hills. And Johnny?"

"He's gone, thank God. I'm remarried to a wonderful man, Steve."

"That warms my heart, Tracy." Maggie whispered, "He was no good."

"I know… I know. I just can't thank you enough. I would never have had the courage to divorce Johnny if it wasn't for you."

Maggie waved off the compliment. "Oh, I'm just a hot-tempered old woman – he got my "Irish" up as they say."

Tracy grasped her hand hard, staring into her eyes. "You don't understand – you were the only one who cared – and cared enough to actually step in. I can never repay you."

A small, trim man with neat dark hair walked over to them. "So this is the Maggie who saved you, Honey?"

Tracy interrupted. "This is my husband, Steve Henderson."

He and Maggie shook hands. "You're a legend," he told Maggie.

She blushed. "A legend?"

"The Avenging Angel who KO'd Johnny Burrows, something I would have liked to have done myself."

Maggie studied him. He looked kind and secure, unlike Johnny. Tracy was obviously happy, looking nothing like the sad-faced girl of old. Maybe the "Napoleonic Complex" theory was wrong.

Steve said, "Oh, sorry about your loss. I heard Eamon was a fine man."

"The best," said Maggie. She turned to Tracy. "And what about Little Johnny and Linda?"

"John is a senior at Central. He'll be going to Pitt next year. Linda is a junior at Sacred Heart. She's looking at colleges. You saved their lives too."

"Oh, no…" said Maggie, embarrassed at such compliments.

Tracy addressed her with a firmness Maggie had never seen from her, no longer Johnny's mousy doormat. "Maggie, don't deny it. It was you – you who cared enough to do something."

Maggie pondered this. "Well, Eamon always told me I had a big heart."

"And a punch to match," said Steve.

THE END

HEROES

IT WAS A cold January day in Pittsburgh, 1963. My mother and I took a bus downtown. (The bus stop was closer to our house than the streetcar.) She wanted to buy me a new sport coat during the post-Christmas sales. It was cold walking down Sixth Street toward Gimbel's. It was always windy downtown, the wind whipping through the valleys between the tall buildings. I was excited because the hot new heavyweight contender Cassius Clay was in town for a fight with Charley Powell at the Civic Arena. The brash, quick-handed "Louisville Lip" was moving up the rankings, as skilled at self-promotion as at boxing. I hoped we might see him. We weren't far from the Arena. My mother thought it was possible, too. Magical things seemed to happen around her, so if she thought we might, we might. As we approached the big revolving doors at Gimbel's, we heard – and saw – a commotion about one block further down the street. A small crowd was forming around a group of black men, near the William Penn Hotel. It was him! Taller than the rest, talking non-stop.

"Mom, can we?" I pleaded.

"Sure, Honey."

We walked quickly toward them. It didn't seem so cold any more. I heard him, his high-pitched voice soaring. "I'm so pretty! Ain't never been hit 'cause I'm so fast!"

He turned his head to show a handsome profile.

"Hey Cassius! What about Sonny Liston?" yelled a man in a gray overcoat.

"That big ugly bear… I'll whup him like his Daddy did! I am the Greatest!!!"

He was surrounded by an entourage of stern black men, looking vigilant and protective. They moved on, only Cassius smiling, as I watched in awe.

"Well, that was pretty good," said my mother as we walked back toward Gimbel's.

"Yeah, pretty cool," I said, getting cold again.

"He sure looks confident. Handsome for a colored fellow, too," she said.

"Yeah, just ask him," I said.

I had been star-struck for over a year. Cassius Clay was not only faster than all the other heavyweights, he even called the round in which he would knock out his opponents. He had just stopped Archie Moore in four rounds in November. Archie was old, but he was a great fighter I had seen on TV on the Friday night fights. The twenty-one-year-old Clay had toyed with him and then knocked him out.

He said Powell would fall in three rounds – and he did. A neighbor, Mr. Hogan, who had seen many live boxing bouts, attended the fight and told me that Clay had the fastest hands he had ever seen.

It was a time of charismatic figures, and at an impressionable age I had seen one in the flesh. The man who defined charisma, John F. Kennedy, had been my hero since that magical year of 1960, when he was elected the first Catholic President and the Pirates won the World Series. Pope John XIII, grandfatherly kind, reigned over our church as "Good Pope John" or "Papa Giovanni." The Beatles came on the scene, with a magic that had girls screaming in ecstasy and boys wishing they could be John, Paul, George, or even Ringo.

In the fall of 1963 I entered eighth grade at St. Bede, and all was right with the world. Good Pope John had died in June, but JFK ruled with unprecedented charisma. Our football team, on which I played tackle, tied heavily favored St. Rosalia for the conference championship. I had many good friends, both male and female, at school. Most of our class had been together throughout grade school, and had grown close.

My mother told me that the three most important positions in the world were Pope, President of the United States, and heavyweight champion, in that order. We had had great ones for the first two, and the third was about to pass to "The Greatest," so I hoped.

I told my classmates that Clay would win the heavyweight title. Not a single one agreed with me. Sonny Liston was the champ. He had won the title from Floyd Patterson in September of 1962 by a spectacular first round knockout, and demolished him again in July of 1963 in one round. Clay, meanwhile, struggled to a decision win against Doug Jones in March. It was the first time his called round prediction failed. In June he got back on track with a called fifth-round TKO of British champion Henry Cooper. The fight with Liston was set for February 25, 1964.

In November came the great tragedy of JFK's assassination. The nation was heartbroken. The handsome young President was succeeded by dumpy-looking Lyndon Baines Johnson. Good Pope John had given way to Paul VI, a serious but decidedly uncharismatic man. The mighty had fallen. Pope Paul VI, LBJ, and surly Sonny Liston comprised the triumvirate of fame. The world desperately needed a Clay win.

Throughout the weeks leading up to the Clay-Liston fight, I predicted a Clay win. Everyone thought I was crazy, except my mother. She saw the confidence in him, and assured me he would win. I touted his speed, skill, and height (two inches taller than Liston) and even imitated his speech. "I'm so pretty. I'm gonna whup that big ugly bear so bad."

The odds makers made Liston an 8-1 favorite. I didn't care. I bet Joey Beckett 25 cents straight up. It was a lot of money for a thirteen-year-old in 1964. He and the rest of my classmates saw it as easy money for him.

On Sunday, February 9, the Beatles appeared on the Ed Sullivan show, sending America's teens into frenzy. Charisma was back – palpable, pulsating. Clay took on Liston in Miami on Tuesday, February 25. My mother and I listened to it on the radio, sitting on her and my dad's bed. My dad was a boxing fan, but had little interest in this one. He saw it as a mismatch.

As we listened, I was very nervous. The menacing Liston was fresh off of two consecutive first round knockouts. It sounded like Clay was moving around the ring a lot. "That's what he has to do," my mother told me. "Jab him from a distance and not get too close, like Billy Conn against Joe Louis."

It sounded like he was doing well. After each round I breathed a sigh of relief. After the sixth round there was a great commotion and confusion among the announcers. Liston was not coming out for the seventh round – Clay had won! I hugged my mother as Clay shouted at the radio audience. *"I shocked the world! I must be the greatest!"* He had indeed, and the world had a new champion.

My friends at school were amazed at my prescience. Beckett paid up, and said with respect, "You know your boxing." To my mind, it was more my mother's mystical intuition than my knowledge. My Clay imitation was more in demand. "I whupped him so bad – ain't that good?"

Shortly after his victory, Clay said he was a "Black Muslim," and changed his name to "Cassius X," like Malcolm X. Many saw it as repudiation of America. The Black Muslims believed that all whites were devils. I didn't care. He was still "The Greatest." I had a gnawing fear that another hero would fall, like JFK and Pope John, not by death, but by a backlash for his beliefs.

One day at school my friend Davey Mento and I passed a note back and forth. He pretended to be Liston, and I pretended to be Clay, who now went by "Muhammad Ali."

Davey: I'll whip you good next time, you loudmouth jerk.

Me: You big ugly bear. I'll whup you like last time.

Davey: Filthy Black Muslim!

Me: There is no God but Allah, and Muhammad is his prophet.

Davey: You're the biggest jagoff in this whole f------ world. (You bastard)

We were both laughing. Sister Miriam, our eighth-grade teacher and the school principal, heard us and walked back to us. "Give me that," she commanded.

I gave it to her, hoping she'd just throw it away. She looked at it briefly, and said, "Both of you see me in my office after class."

At the end of class, we followed her to her small office at the landing between the first and second floors. She gave us the note, and said, "I want each of you to read what you wrote."

This was not good. Sister Miriam was new that year, brought in to be the principal and teach eighth graders. She was younger (late twenties), sterner, and smarter than the other nuns. She was tall and slim with quick movements. In her swishing black habit with starched white collar that covered her hair, neck, and ears, only her face from forehead to just below the chin showed. We were sprouting eighth-graders, but she could look us right in the eye. Her exposed face showed penetrating gray eyes, clear skin, a straight nose, and full lips. She was pretty, even with wire rim glasses and no makeup. Her clear, strong voice exuded confidence. She had "gravitas." With most of the dowdy, child-loving nuns at our school, we older boys could half-charm, half-trick them into letting us slide on most transgressions. Not so with Sister Miriam – she could not be charmed or deluded.

Davey began, "I'll whip you good next time, you loudmouth jerk."

I answered, "You big ugly bear. I'll whup you like last time."

We both read in a slow monotone. We could not laugh. She would kill us. It didn't sound as funny reading it to her.

"Filthy Black Muslim," said Davey.

"There is no God but Allah and Muhammad is his pro..."

She interrupted me, "That's a fine profession of faith for a Catholic boy."

"Sister, I was just pretending..." THWACK!

She slapped me across the face – hard. It stung. She looked at Davey, who was hesitating.

"Proceed."

He read, "You're the biggest..." he said "jerk" instead of "jagoff." He stopped. She glared at him. He continued, "... in this whole..." He had written "f------"which obviously meant "fucking." He hesitated again. She nodded to him, and he said, "...in this whole *fanatical* world."

Good substitute, I thought. He couldn't say the last part, "You bastard." He didn't get slapped. She was more offended by my "profession of faith" than by his swear words.

"You will take this and have it signed by both of your fathers. I want it on my desk tomorrow."

I took it home. My dad read it and actually laughed, but said, "Don't be passing notes in class." I never told him that I got slapped. He might have thought that I did something more serious. He took it to Dr. Mento, who also signed it. Both fathers were more concerned with our lack of respect in class than with the actual content of the note. But that was the end of it.

CASSIUS CLAY – Cassius X – Muhammad Ali became a great champion, even a charismatic figure in American history. He was stripped of his title in 1967 for refusing to serve in the military during the unpopular Vietnam War, an act of courage. He was banned from boxing for three years, until 1970. He returned with the same flare, but my hero worship waned. His braggadocio became cruel taunting of overmatched opponents at times, and he disdained good sportsmanship. Yet there was always a twinkle in his eye, like he was putting us on.

Later in life I learned that the Clay-Liston spectacle that had so enthralled me was probably fixed. The mob-owned Liston likely threw the fight so that the mob could make money betting on his opponent.

I also learned that JFK was a reckless adulterer, not the Knight in Shining Armor I had envisioned. But he was still the first Irish Catholic President, a symbol of arrival for my tribe.

I still look back fondly on those days of charismatic heroes: the handsome knight of Camelot, the flashy young boxer, the Good Pope, and the Fab Four. But other heroes were less famous, and closer: a strong father, a mystical, loving mother, and devoted nuns... even the tough one.

THE END

HAMMERS OF JUSTICE

AS THE ST. Bede parishioners filed in for the 9:15 Mass, some heard the whispering. *The statues are missing! Someone said they were stolen!*

Whispered rumors of the theft of two of the "Three Kings" statues spread throughout the church. Just before Mass began, Father Dimerski announced, "As you may have noticed, two of our statues have been stolen. The police are investigating. For now, let us pray for their safe return and for the misguided thieves who took them."

The life-sized outdoor Nativity scene was a beautiful, charming tradition at St. Bede. The pastor, Father Maloney, had spent a small fortune for it. Every December, head janitor Chuck Phelan and his assistants set it up between the church and Rectory. The set included color-painted, cast-stone statues of Joseph, Mary, Jesus, a shepherd, a lamb, a donkey, and an ox that were set inside a wooden stable with real straw strewn about the floor. It was a popular site to visit and say a few prayers. On Christmas Eve, Baby Jesus miraculously appeared in his little crib. The three kings were the most elaborately colored. They appeared on the lawn in front of the church on Christmas Day. Each day Chuck moved them a little closer to the stable, where they were scheduled to arrive on the Feast of the Epiphany, twelve days after Christmas.

Early this Sunday morning, December 29, 1963, Chuck discovered that two of the kings were gone. He couldn't imagine who would do such a thing – certainly not any St. Bede parishioner. He notified Father Maloney, who called the police. They came and took down the information, and promised they would look into it. They said it could be professionals looking to sell them for money, or just some punk kids pulling a stupid prank. As heavy as the statues were, it would require at least two perpetrators.

Chuck had been head janitor at St. Bede for thirty years, but he had never seen anything like this. An occasional broken window at the school or theft of petty cash from the poor box had been the worst crimes at St. Bede. The theft of the statues was a major crime, and Chuck somehow felt responsible.

Chuck recalled the day he began work at St. Bede. He had gone to grade school there, and knew Father Maloney, who had been the first and only pastor. It was in the 1930's during the Great Depression, and jobs were hard to find. Chuck was walking down Dallas Avenue to catch a bus to East Pittsburgh to apply for a job at the big Westinghouse plant. He didn't have much hope. He saw Father Maloney sitting on the Rectory porch and they struck up a conversation. Father Maloney said to him, "Why don't you work for me? I could use a good handyman and janitor."

Chuck took the job and never looked back. For thirty years now he had done the maintenance, cleaning, and fixing of anything and everything at St. Bede church and school, located just a few blocks from his home. Now he even had a part-time assistant or two, depending on the work load. Although short and slim, Chuck was strong and energetic, and enjoyed the work. He even served Mass when he was needed. He felt he was doing God's work. Now in his fifties, Chuck still had the impish grin that never left his face. He was always smiling and willing to help. He had a receding hairline, and on the right side of his forehead he had a large, protruding birthmark that looked like a reddish-brown "bubble." It was about the size of a golf ball, and it looked like a reddish stone had been embedded in his head. He had been self-conscious about it as a kid, but at this age never gave it a second thought. The school kids called him "Chuck the Bubble," but never to his face. They all knew him and greeted him as "Chuck," the friendly janitor who always seemed to have a hammer, a screwdriver, or a mop. He was as much a constant in their lives as the black-clad Sisters of St. Joseph, who taught them.

MAX SCHILLING WAS a Pittsburgh city policeman. He patrolled the Point Breeze neighborhood in which St. Bede was located. He often walked the beat, especially the "over the hill" section, the western part of Point Breeze near Mellon Park. (Point Breeze is bisected by a hill that rises from Dallas Avenue for one block up to Linden, and down another block to Hastings. Those from the eastern part of Point Breeze around St. Bede and

Frick Park call the western part "over the hill," as in "He's from over the hill." What do those from the western part call the eastern part? "Over the hill" also. But as St. Bede is the traditional focal point of the neighborhood, those from that eastern area feel that the other section near Mellon Park is more properly "over the hill" from what really matters.)

Max had been a professional boxer in the 1930's, and his face showed it. The great champion Billy Conn, now a neighbor, was fond of saying "Maxie would take five punches to land one." His nose was smashed in from hundreds of rounds in the ring. He had scar tissue around his eyes, visible even through his glasses, and "cauliflower ears." One look at Max and a person knew instantly that he had been a professional boxer. His face told the story.

As a boxer, Max won some and lost some. His claim to fame was that he had once gone the distance with Tony Zale, who later became middle-weight champion and a Hall-of-Famer. Max lost a unanimous decision that night, but proved he was tough – Zale couldn't knock him out. Max may have taken five punches for every one landed, but, oh, what that one could do. If Max landed his right, it would hurt his opponent. Several times in his long career as a police officer he had felled an unsuspecting criminal with a punch. The newspapers liked to call it the "Hammer of Justice," as was written in one article's headline:

EX PUG MAX SCHILLING QUELLS GANG FIGHT WITH
"HAMMER OF JUSTICE"

The neighborhood kids all knew Max and greeted him with "Hi Maxie!" He would smile and wave. They referred to him as "Max the Cop."

Max was puzzled and disturbed about the theft at St. Bede, and decided to watch the place more carefully. A taste of success could bring the thieves back for more.

St. Bede Church had never been locked, even at night. The priests believed that access for visitation and prayer should always be available. Chuck Phelan worried about the valuables in the church, especially the

indoor statues of St. Joseph and the Blessed Mother, and the gold tabernacle. Would anyone dare to steal from God? Nowadays, who knew? If
they could assassinate President Kennedy, as was done this past November,
anything was possible.

Two days later the statues were found in Frick Park, smashed into
a thousand tiny pieces. The verdict was in. It was not professionals, it was
vicious punks.

"Chuck the Bubble" was angry. Punks had perpetrated a major crime
on his watch. "Max the Cop" was angry. Punks had perpetrated a major
crime on *his* watch.

Chuck took to spending long hours after work at St. Bede. He was
afraid to leave the place. Late one night he saw a car with five young men
circle the block several times. Could they be the ones? He hid in the sacristy of the church and waited. He heard the big church front door open.
Peeking through the sacristy door, he saw four of the men enter the church,
while one waited outside in the car. They were scruffy, and around 18 to 20
years old. He didn't recognize any of them. He snuck back to the phone in
the school office and called the police.

Max heard the radio call and headed for St. Bede. He knew he should
wait for backup, but that was something he rarely did. His "Hammer of
Justice" was backup enough. Max pulled up at the church, his siren silent.
The getaway driver saw him, panicked, and pulled away. As Max entered
St. Bede, he saw two of the men carrying the gold tabernacle down the
center aisle. "Hold it right there," he told them. He didn't draw his gun. He
wouldn't need it for these punks. They set the tabernacle down. Suddenly,
the other two jumped Max from behind, wrestling him to the ground. The
first two began kicking Max in the face and body. He struggled to keep
hold of his gun. Max wouldn't quit struggling. They couldn't control him.
They continued to kick at him viciously. Then they started falling… one…
two… three.

Chuck the Bubble had conked three of them on the head from behind
with his own "Hammer of Justice," a real hammer. They fell to the ground,

groggy. Chuck's impish grin was as wide as it could stretch. He saved the last punk for Max, and watched in joyous anticipation. Max pushed the kid off of him, and then grabbed him and propped him up. The kid had a look of terror on his face. This middle-aged man that the four of them could not subdue now had him one – to – one. Max dreamed that he was in the ring again, taking five punches to land one, bleeding from the nose and mouth. The "Hammer of Justice" crashed into the jaw of the last punk. He was unconscious before he hit the ground. Chuck couldn't stifle a deep belly laugh. He and Max shook hands.

The newspapers loved it. The *Pittsburgh Press* article the next day was headlined:

EX-PUG MAX SCHILLING AND ST. BEDE JANITOR WIELD
"HAMMERS OF JUSTICE" TO FOIL ROBBERY ATTEMPT

They had a picture of Max and Chuck side-by-side, with Chuck holding up his hammer and Max holding up his right fist.

The "hammered" punks squealed on the getaway driver, and all five were eventually sentenced to jail terms. It was a happy ending, but both Chuck and Max were troubled. As they neared the ends of their careers, an age of innocence was ending. The President had been assassinated. Thieves were brazen enough to steal holy objects from a church. The world was changing.

THE END

DUSTY

JOHNNY DORSEY COULD hardly believe his good luck. When Sister Hilary shuffled the seating arrangement after the second report card period, he ended up right behind Joann Kelly, the new girl. He thought she was the prettiest one in his eighth grade class, and now he would get to know her. She had made quite a splash when she began school at St. Bede in September, capturing the attention of all the eighth grade boys with her good looks and graceful manner. Even the high school boys were aware of her presence in the neighborhood.

Not only was she the prettiest one in Johnny's mind, she also looked "different." St. Bede was a mix of Irish, German, and Italian Catholics or various blends thereof, and all looked the part. He knew a lot of good-looking girls, but Joann was exotic in his eyes. Although her last name was Kelly, she didn't look Irish. She had high cheekbones and a dark complexion, always looking like she had a tan. She dressed in cute jumpers and blouse-skirt combinations that showed her trim figure. But her bright green eyes attracted Johnny the most. She had long lashes and wore more eye liner and shadow than the other girls. Now he could watch her from behind all day.

She was friendly with some of the girls, but didn't seem to have a best friend or clique. She was still too new for that. The boys tried to show off or flirt with her. She was polite, but somewhat aloof, not allowing any one boy to get too close. Her school behavior was good. She rarely talked in class and didn't chew gum. She obeyed Sister's directives and did her homework. When called on in class she struggled at times. She appeared to be an average student at best. Johnny was smart, and hoped he could help her.

For the first few days he spoke little to her, just a polite "Hello" or "Hey." He would be low-key like her, so she would grow to trust him. If he leaned forward he could smell her hair without her knowing it.

One day he brought in a pack of wild cherry cough drops and offered her two. Although no candy or gum or food of any kind was permitted in class, she accepted them gratefully and smiled at him. Johnny thought his heart would melt. When Sister Hilary left the room and they waited for the music teacher, she turned around and said, "Umm... these are good." She was close enough that he could smell the cough drops from her mouth. Her voice was "different" too, lower and slightly raspy, which Johnny found sexy. The cough drops became a regular treat.

Joann slowly made friends among the girls, and got invited to parties. She could do the Twist or Frug decently, but was not a top dancer like some of the girls. She danced with a variety of boys. She was not interested in "pairing off" like some others. Johnny soon found out why. She was the "girlfriend" of Tommy Johnson, a junior in high school. "TJ" had been a star football player at St. Bede, and one of the "coolest" kids, popular with both sexes. Johnny's heart sank at the news, but it did not surprise him that Joann could get someone like that, with her exotic good looks. At the parties he always danced a slow dance with Joann, holding her tight, enticed by the smell of her hair and perfume. She held tight too, but never in the wrap-around, neck-kissing style of kids who were "going steady." She limited him – and others – to one or two slow dances, ending with a friendly "Thank you." Johnny laughed to himself at what TJ would do if he knew what Johnny was thinking as he held Joann. *He'd kick my ass.*

The eighth-graders had their favorite dance tunes and artists. Chubby Checker's Twist tunes were still popular, as were the newer Beatles and Dave Clark Five. Johnny and Joann both liked the soulful, haunting voice of Dusty Springfield, not easy to dance to but beautiful for rhapsodizing. Her "Wishin' and Hopin'," "Stay Awhile," and I Only Wanna Be With You" had words that made Johnny wish and hope to be with Joann. He knew she didn't feel the same, but he could fantasize.

In class they began talking a good bit. One day she asked if he could come to her house after school to help with homework. He was glad to do it, although he knew it was only as a "friend." She talked often of TJ and his car, and his older friends.

Joann's house was nice, bigger and prettier than the one Johnny lived in. It had expensive furniture, beautiful drapes, and a nice smell. Joann lived there with her divorced mother. As the homework visits became frequent, Johnny noticed that her mother was almost never home. He asked her about it.

"Oh, my mom's always out showing houses. She's a real estate agent. Dad lives in Chicago. I don't see him much."

Johnny got a glimpse of Mrs. Kelly once. She stopped in to change clothes. Joann introduced them. "Mom, this is my friend Johnny Dorsey, the one who helps me with homework." Johnny wished she had said "boyfriend" instead of "friend."

Mrs. Kelly wore an elegant black dress with gold earrings and several shiny rings and bracelets. Her grooming was meticulous, with stylish hair, nails, and makeup. She was quite sociable. "Nice to meet you, young man. Thank you for helping Joann with her homework. She needs to take it more seriously."

Johnny could tell right away that Mrs. Kelly was different from the other moms he knew in Point Breeze. For one thing, she worked. Most of the moms he knew stayed at home with a bunch of kids while the dads went to work. Mrs. Kelly had an air of independence about her, like someone in the business world. Tall with erect posture and a firm handshake, she looked like she could hold her own in a world of men. And he could see where Joann got her looks. Mrs. Kelly was tall and dark like Joann, with brown eyes and black hair. Joann had lighter eyes and hair than her mom, but the same high cheekbones. Johnny thought that Joann had a prettier face.

Mrs. Kelly left quickly, driving off in her white Thunderbird.

The progress with homework was slow. Joann liked to joke around rather than concentrate on the work. She loved to listen to records and talk about music, which they did on their frequent breaks.

"I love Dusty Springfield," said Joann. "She can sing, she's cool, she knows how to dress and wear makeup."

Johnny liked her singing, but thought the makeup was a bit much. Springfield wore heavy eye makeup, with elongated and blackened eyelashes both above and below the eyes, and eyelids black. But that was what

Joann liked, and imitated, although not as extreme as Springfield. Her mother permitted it, to Johnny's surprise. It did give her an alluring look.

"She has a cool name, too," Joann continued. "I wish I had a cool name like Lisa or Wendy, instead of plain old Joann. TJ calls me 'Jo-Jo,' which I hate."

"Why don't you tell him you hate it?"

"I don't tell TJ anything. He tells me."

Johnny thought of the eye makeup similarities, and said, "I think I'll call you Dusty. You look like her, except prettier."

Joann, a little surprised, tilted her head in thought. "I like it… Dusty. Yeah, you can call me Dusty. It will be our secret."

She smiled at him. Johnny felt closer to her than ever.

One Friday afternoon, Johnny and "Dusty" were listening to records. She had quickly tired of homework. They heard a commotion outside as a black Cadillac pulled in front of the house. TJ jumped out of it and headed for the front door. He burst in.

"Hey, Jo-Jo! I got my dad's car for a while. Let's go for a ride!"

She ran to TJ's arms. He hugged and kissed her, which she loved. Johnny's heart sank. TJ looked at Johnny. "Eh, little Johnny Dorsey. What's new, kid?"

"He was helping me with my homework," Joann said.

"Time to hit the road, kid," said TJ. "Come on, Jo-Jo. Let's ride!"

Joann turned to Johnny. "Bye, Johnny. I'll see you in school Monday."

As he walked home, Johnny lamented his fate. How could he compete with that?" TJ was 16, he could drive, he could get his dad's Cadillac. He was in high school, he was cool. That's what girls liked. Johnny was only a "friend."

The following week at school he told Dusty that he was busy and couldn't help her. She was still friendly and turned around often to talk to him. Her charms were hard to resist – he joked and laughed with her. He continued to supply her with cough drops. But he kept finding excuses not to help her with her homework. He had to draw the line somewhere.

Two weeks later she came in on Monday looking distressed. She had very little eye makeup on, and looked like she was ready to cry. She was silent and somber all day. He didn't bother her. The next day was the same. She spoke to no one. Just before dismissal, she turned around and said,

"Johnny… I need your help. Please come over after school. I really need for you to."

Her eyes locked with his, pleading with him. He had never seen her so serious. That was more than he could resist, and he agreed. He was surprised that she cared so much about the school work.

As they walked to her house, she was silent. She did, however, accept cough drops without speaking. They entered her house. No one was home, as usual.

"How's the math?" he asked.

She dropped her books on the dining room table and looked him straight in the eye.

"I don't care about the homework. I… I need someone to talk to. You're the only friend I have."

"What about TJ – or your mom?"

She looked down, tears falling from the pretty eyelashes.

"TJ… he…" She stopped, shaking her head in frustration. She took Johnny's hand.

"Let's go outside."

They sat at the top of the front porch steps, side by side. His view of her face – the elegant cheekbones, the whites of her eyes against tan, flushed cheeks, the tear-laden eyelashes – warmed his heart. He felt he had never seen anything so beautiful. She stared ahead, pensive.

"What's wrong?" he said softly, moving closer to her.

She turned to him, pretty wet eyes wide, and started to sob. She put her arms around him, pressing her wet cheeks against his.

"He… made me… go all the way… right here in my own house." She cried into his shoulder.

Johnny resisted the impulse to say *What did you expect? Isn't that what you wanted?*

Instead he said, "Oh Dusty. That bastard."

"I'm only thirteen," she sobbed. She held her face in her hands, crying softly. Johnny didn't know what to say. He thought for a while, and then said,

"Let's hope you don't get pregnant."

"He used a... rubber... so I guess I won't." She squeezed him hard, groaning. "Oh, it's worse... much worse... *horrible*."

She cried again, her face in her hands. Johnny again didn't know what to say. He had never encountered such distress. He tried to soothe her. "It'll be OK."

She turned her head quickly to him. "You can't tell anyone."

"No, I won't."

"There's... more." She froze, looking like she had swallowed an egg.

"What do you mean?"

She took a deep breath, summoning the courage to tell him. She spoke in a monotone.

"His friend – Halloran – was with him. TJ made him watch us. I kept saying 'No! No!' but he was too strong. They were both laughing. I felt... like a whore." She cried, "I can't believe he would do that to me!"

Johnny held her tight. "Oh, Dusty. You poor girl." He felt an intense hatred for TJ.

She continued, "Then he asked... if Halloran... could... do it to me too. I just screamed so hysterically – I wouldn't stop – that they both left."

She buried her head in his shoulder and cried, deep sobs. He kissed the top of her head, just letting her cry. For a long time they sat in silence.

A black Cadillac pulled up slowly and stopped in front of the house. TJ got out, looking somber. "Jo-Jo baby, I've been calling you. How come you won't answer the phone? I want to tell you how sorry I am." He walked to the bottom of the steps.

"Dorsey! Time to hit the road, kid."

Johnny didn't move. TJ pleaded,

"I'm sorry, baby. Sorry for being such an asshole."

"You got that right!" Johnny blurted out.

TJ leaped up the steps and grabbed Johnny. "Time to go - now!"

TJ pushed him toward the steps. Johnny swung his fist, which the taller TJ easily blocked. He grabbed Johnny's neck and threw him face first to the porch floor, screaming "Now get the fuck out of here before I have to hurt you!"

"Bastard!" Johnny screamed, diving at his legs. TJ grabbed Johnny by the shoulders and brought a knee up hard into his gut. Johnny rolled on the floor in great pain, unable to stand.

TJ put his arms around Joann. "Baby. I am so sorry. I promise you – it will never happen again."

She pulled away from him, crying. She ran into the bathroom and locked the door. TJ banged on the door, to no avail. He calmed down, and came over to Johnny. "Eh! Dorsey! Sorry kid. I didn't want to. You want a ride home?"

"No," Johnny answered, and left. While he was walking, the Cadillac slowed down next to him and honked. TJ said, "Come on, kid. Get in."

Johnny ignored him.

AT SCHOOL DUSTY barely spoke to anyone. Johnny still brought her cough drops, which she accepted. He asked if she needed help with homework, but she declined. A few weeks later Sister Hilary shuffled the seats again, and he was far from Dusty. They drifted apart, with little or no interaction from that point.

MONTHS LATER, ON a warm May night, TJ's black Cadillac drove by and honked. Johnny saw Dusty riding shotgun. Their eyes locked. Her makeup was heavier than ever. Johnny thought she looked sad. He walked to the drug store and bought a pack of wild cherry cough drops.

THE END

FIRST FIGHT

THE GRAY OF evening was settling over the smoky little town along the Monongahela River. Just off the main street, stood the old high school gymnasium, tonight bustling with activity. Inside, its wooden bleachers creaked as the packed-in patrons, mostly male, fidgeted in their seats. The opening bout was late.

Finally, the first two combatants came striding down opposite aisles with their seconds. The young fighters jerked with nervous energy; the aged seconds were calm and businesslike. Mike Miller surveyed the crowd as he approached the ring at the center of the gym. He could see many of his friends from Point Breeze. He caught a glimpse of his dad, mom, and sister. He knew Mom would be praying. He didn't want to disappoint them. It was his boxing debut, and he fought to suppress his own second-guessing. It was too late to turn back now. *Think positively!* Cigar smoke wafted through his nostrils. Many in the crowd had the leathery, scarred-eyebrow faces of aging ex-boxers. They were part of the strange boxing subculture that attended these events, turned on by the prospect of a vigorous battle between two young warriors. But bloodthirsty they were not. Their most salient emotion was respect. Respect – even reverence – for the style, the technique, the conditioning. But most of all for the bravery.

Mike looked resplendent in his black-lettered white robe: fresh-faced, with wavy brown hair brushed straight back. His tall, lean body towered over the middle-aged men carrying the water bucket and equipment: bottle, sponge, Vaseline, tape – all the tools of the trade. Together they walked up the ring steps, ducked through the ropes, and then fear struck.

What am I doing here? This is crazy! A silly, romantic notion about a primitive sport that's going to result in brain damage. Fight it! Fight it! Don't think of such things now! Please get it started before my stomach melts – God help me!

Thoughts flashed of his friend and sparring partner Kerry Jones, *Poor Kerry!* Who had similarly debuted last month. Kerry seemed to freeze with nervousness at the start of the bout, and was brutally battered until the referee stopped it before the end of the first round. *How embarrassing!*

What if it happens to me? What if I get cut – or knocked down? Kerry had not returned to the gym since then, despite encouraging words from other fighters. Mike was determined not to let the same thing happen to him.

Fortunately Mike was able to convey a relaxed outward appearance, while inner fears and doubts singed his brain cells. He shadow-boxed vigorously in the ring, while the seconds set up shop in the assigned corner. Then the panic subsided and his thoughts shifted to his first venture into the old Lou Belker Gym on Franklin Street.

He hesitated as he approached the big iron door, then took a deep breath, opened it, and walked in. He was immediately hit by the rat-a-tat-tat of speed bags, jump ropes scraping the floor, and grunting fighters pounding the heavy bag. Trainers yelled instructions. A musty smell of sweat and Right Guard hung in the air. Then a bell rang and everything stopped. All eyes seemed to be on Mike.

"Is Lou here?" he asked.

A distinguished looking elderly man stepped forward.

"You must be Miller."

Mike nodded.

"Yeah, kid, Johnny told me about you. Come on over here and let Andy fix you up."

A smallish, Italian-looking guy with a thin moustache motioned to follow him into the back room. As Mike followed, Lou, who was obviously in charge of the place, lightly grabbed the slight coat of fat on Mike's stomach and barked "Whaddya – some kind of cake eater?"

"Yeah, sometimes, I guess," said Mike shyly.

Lou faked a friendly right to Mike's ribs, and then dismissed him with mock scorn. After a one minute rest the bell rang again and the noise started back up. Everything in Lou's Gym happened in alternating three- and one-minute periods, marked by a loud automatic bell.

Mike's pleasant daydream was abruptly interrupted by the announcer, who told the fighters to go to their respective corners. He tapped the microphone, and welcomed the crowd to an evening of boxing.

The gym darkened except for the bright lights above the ring. Mike's stomach churned furiously and his cheeks felt hot. There was nowhere to run.

"...and in this corner, in his first fight, weighing one hundred and sixty-five pounds, from the Lou Belker Gym, MIKE MIL – LER!"

Rude reality. Daydreaming was more fun.

The referee brought both fighters and their seconds to the center of the ring. "I want a clean fight. No hittin' below the belt line, no head butts. Listen to my commands. When I tell you to stop, stop. Now go back to your corners. When the bell rings, let's give these fans a good fight. Good Luck to both of yins!"

Mike walked back to his corner with Lou, who massaged his upper back and whispered, "It's just like in the gym. Do like you've been taught."

Andy touched his shoulder, "He's all yours, Mike."

Mike looked across the ring into his opponent's eyes, which were fiercely staring back. A chill ran up his spine. Then, strangely, a dreamlike calm settled over him, just before the bell rang. CLANG! "St. Michael the Archangel, protect us in battle," he whispered to himself. His mother had told him to say that.

Mike approached his opponent, determined to keep his wits about him. *Jab, stay calm, remember what you were taught.* He had seen so many fighters lose composure and start swinging wildly as soon as the action heated up. The opponent had a tough-looking, determined face, topped by coarse, black-curly hair. Despite his tough look, Mike noticed that his build was no more impressive than Mike's. *You don't fight with your face.* Mike felt that he was in the best shape of his life. His stomach had hardened up to show visible muscles. The "cake-eater" fat was only a memory. He could go hard for round after round on the heavy bag, the speed bag, and the rope.

The fighters circled one another. Mike shot a nervous long-range jab that fell short. The opponent moved in, and both fighters threw a flurry of hard, awkward punches that connected on each other's gloves and shoulders.

"Jab!" yelled Lou. "Stick and move!"

Mike landed a jab flush on the nose, but the opponent waded in and fired a right and left to the ribs. Mike tried a left hook and missed, threw the right, and then *Whack!* got tagged with a smashing right to the nose followed by two good shots to the head. All the training went out the window as Mike fired back furiously, stepping into a whirlwind of punches. *This was war!* Both fighters degenerated into undisciplined fury, missing most punches but landing some, with Mike's opponent definitely getting the better of it. Mike felt intense hatred for that tough face in front of him, wanting with all his heart to pound it into a purple mess. Then the bell rang, snapping him back to reality. He had survived the first round. He walked back to the corner to a cacophonous verbal barrage.

"Mike! Jab the guy! Stick! Move! Double jab! Then throw your right! You're losin' control of yourself!"

He had heard Lou and Andy yelling during the round, but he didn't hear what they were saying in the heat of the action.

The ten-second warning whistle blew; they popped his mouthpiece back in. Mike had been hit a lot in the first round, but he felt okay. Apparently his opponent wasn't a devastating knockout puncher. The bell rang for Round Two. Mike was determined to stay under control and use the skills he had been taught. He walked right at the opponent and threw a double jab, the first one blocked, the second hitting the face clean and hard. The opponent backed up momentarily, then waded in with two punches that missed. Mike set up nicely and threw the double jab again, hitting both, then followed with a hard right to the forehead that rocked his opponent's head back. Things were going to be different this round! Mike stayed under good control throughout, landing many jabs and an occasional right, while the opponent landed only a few good shots to the body. Mike could hear Lou and Andy's relentless yells, which had taken a triumphal, even jubilant tone.

"YOU GOT 'IM, MIKIE BABY! YOU GOT 'IM!" screamed Andy.

"Thatsa way to fight, Mike! Keep jabbin' – double jab like I taught ya!" barked the deep, reassuring voice of Lou Belker, who'd been through many a battle like this.

Lou was a beloved icon of the local boxing scene. He didn't look like a typical trainer or ex-boxer. He was tall, slim, and distinguished looking, with deep set brown eyes and graying temples. He had a vaguely patrician air that one would associate more with a doctor or Congressman. The resonant voice conveyed authority and self-assurance. He had boxed in the Army years ago, and had become a student of the game and a talented teacher. He had had a successful career as a plumbing supply salesman, but retired in his mid-fifties to devote full time to his gym. He still dressed often in a coat and tie, especially on fight night. Yet he was readily accepted by the world he had chosen. The grizzled old trainers appreciated his commitment, and saw him as a "class act." The tough young fighters worshipped him. He was the one who owned the gym, bought the equipment, promoted the fight cards, and taught them the manly art. He took an interest in each of his fighters as a person, a kindly father figure who motivated them with sure-fire authority and strength. Mike had come to respect and admire Lou like all the other fighters. A compliment from him produced a warm, glowing feeling that made Mike proud of himself.

CLANG! Round Three – the final round. The referee brought the fighters together to touch gloves, a time-honored boxing tradition. Tough Face came at him like a man possessed. THUD! THWACK! A torrent of punches landed on Mike's forearms and shoulders. He tried to set up and box, but the aggressive fury kept him off balance. There was nothing to do but punch back in kind. The battle escalated as each fighter threw punch after punch in rapid succession. It continued for the whole round. The crowd broke into applause a good thirty seconds before the final round bell, and many rose in appreciation. The bell rang, fighters stopped, and the corner men jumped into the ring to attend them.

"YOU BEAT 'IM MIKE!" screamed Andy above the confusing din.

"No question, my guy won," Lou said loudly in the direction of the three judges working at ringside.

It was all over and Mike felt tingles of pride in his spine and stomach. The applause continued, ringing in his ears. He could see the faces in the crowd, friends and family, iron-jawed ex-fighters, all cheering for him.

Lou continued to work the judges. "MY BOY WON IT!" he kept shouting. Mike felt so grateful to this man who had molded an awkward kid into a competent amateur boxer. All the hard work – the running, the endless sparring sessions, the bag, the rope – seemed well worth it at this proud moment.

The announcer grabbed the microphone and the crowd quieted. Everyone listened anxiously for the decision. Everyone, that is, but Mike. He just smiled. He'd already won the real battle. He was a *fighter* now.

THE END

DADDY'S GIRL

JANET'S FATHER WAS proud of being a Marine. He was a World War II veteran, wounded while storming the beach at Guadalcanal. He still kept in touch with his World War II buddies, attending reunions nearly every year. Every Memorial Day or Veterans Day he was marching somewhere, either with the American Legion or the VFW. His military service was the defining point of his life.

He was the father of three, and his children were important to him. He was a hard man who rarely showed his emotions, but Janet had no doubt of his deep love for his wife and children. She would soon find out how deep it really ran.

He grew up in the Depression in the tough, working-class neighborhood of Lawrenceville. He was loyal to Lawrenceville and boasted about its strong sense of community and faith. She had heard of its famous residents: Stephen Collins Foster, Fritzie Zivic, and Ted Sadowski, among others. She had heard over and over how the neighborhood responded to the nation's wars way out of proportion to its numbers. Men from Lawrenceville were willing to fight and die for their country.

He and his wife Gloria moved to Point Breeze just after Janet, their first child, was born. Although proud of Lawrenceville, her father wanted something better for his children; perhaps the new neighborhood would give them opportunities and exposure he never had.

Everything about John Hellman exuded masculinity and toughness: Marine, Pittsburgh city cop, football coach – even his name. He had boxed and played football in his youth, and he helped coach the local grade school football team. But he had a tender spot in his heart for his children, especially his daughter, Janet. He was tougher on his sons, expecting them to follow in his ways.

Janet felt that "Daddy" (she still called him "Daddy" despite being in her early twenties) treated her like a child. He had always been protective – some boys in high school were afraid to date her – and she knew that no one who knew him would ever harm her, for fear of his wrath. But she was 23 now and a Registered Nurse, working in the ICU at Shadyside

Hospital and taking classes at Pitt to get her Bachelor of Science degree. She was a competent professional who was well-respected by her co-workers. Around her father she felt like a little girl. He couldn't seem to respect her for the accomplished young woman she had become.

Her brothers, Jack and Tommy, had earned their father's grudging approval by doing well in sports. He felt he had to act tough with them and be critical, yet Janet knew how proud he was of them. He boasted of their achievements to his friends and to Janet, but never to the boys themselves. He had to maintain a tough exterior, lest the boys get too complacent. How Janet yearned for that kind of approval from him! She knew she could never compete with what the boys had done in sports.

The social revolutions of the 1960s, especially the Vietnam War protests, were difficult times for John Hellman. It seemed that everything he held sacred was being challenged. "Free love," men wearing their hair long like girls, the glorification of drugs like marijuana and LSD, as well as war protests, were abominations to him. Janet knew to avoid these subjects with him.

Janet's mother, Gloria, was loyal and supportive of her husband's ideas. She played the "good cop" role, allowing John to be the disciplinarian. Her ultimate weapon was the threat to "tell Dad." It worked. Janet could confide in her – to a point. She didn't understand Janet's desire to have a career of her own. She thought it was more important to get married and raise a family. She and John held to the traditional view that a child did not move out of the home until marriage. Janet broached this difficult topic with her.

"Y'know, Mom, I'd like to get my own place... an apartment, close to work.

Gloria looked puzzled. "Why? You have it good here. You'd have to pay rent and utilities. You give me a hundred a month to help out. You'll never find a deal like that."

Janet wrung her hands. "It's too crowded here, with you and Dad and the boys. I need more space – a place where I can be independent. And Mom, I can afford it."

Gloria looked even more puzzled. "This is your family. This is home. You can come and go as you please. You don't need more space."

Janet dropped her head, smiling. "You don't understand…"

"No I don't. What would Dad think?"

Janet paused, careful to quell her rising anger. "What do you think, Mom? What do you think?"

"I told you what I think. And I resent the implication that I only follow what Dad thinks. What I told you is what I think, OK?"

"OK," Janet said quietly, feeling misunderstood. She would get her own apartment, approved or not. They'd get over it.

John frequently stopped at the VFW in Lawrenceville, where his old buddies hung out. At the bar he greeted Pat, the bartender. Only John and one other patron were in the bar. John said, "An Iron for me, and give the hippie kid there whatever he wants."

The "hippie kid" was Larry Conley, son of John's friend Jim Conley, and a Vietnam veteran. Larry wore his thick brown hair long, nearly shoulder-length, and parted it down the middle. John teased him about it.

"At least part it on the side, like a man."

"You wish you had this hair," Larry retorted, referring to John's thinning top.

"If I did, it'd look a lot neater."

John tolerated Larry because he was a vet, one who had seen real action in Vietnam. Larry was tall and well-built, with a pensive look on his face. He wore bell bottom jeans, sandals, and a denim shirt. He had a full Fu Manchu moustache and wire rim glasses. A similarly clad non-vet would not have fared so well in John's presence. But he knew Larry was a good kid from a good family, who was probably going through a phase. They had debated the Vietnam War several times, finding little common ground.

"So what's the latest with the Commie peaceniks?" John asked.

Larry was more serious. "We gotta get outta there, Mr. Hellman. Too many kids getting hurt – and for what?"

John had his frustrations with the war too, but for different reasons. "We gotta win and get out – that's how you get out. The politicians are tying our hands."

"It's not winnable. You can't just destroy a whole country."

John's voice rose. "You put someone like Patton in there and he'd clean up the place in a year."

"Then what? What if the people don't want to be ruled by Patton?"

"They sure as hell don't want to be ruled by Ho Chi Minh."

"Who knows? They seem to fight harder for him than for us."

John took a deep breath. "We need to stop the Communists wherever they are. They want to take over the world, one country at a time. The Russians and Chinese are behind this. I know that sounds ridiculous to you, but it's the Goddamn truth."

"I agree with you."

"You do? About what?"

"That it sounds ridiculous to me."

John shook his head. "Get the hippie another one. Maybe he'll see things more clearly after another beer."

"Let me buy you one, Mr. Hellman. You're always buying for me."

"The old guys buy for the young guys. That's the way it works here."

John paid for the round. Larry awkwardly broached a subject that he felt went to the heart of the matter. "Mr. Hellman… if this war continues… would you want your sons to fight there?"

John had thought of this. "If it was a war we were in to win, yes. My boys will do their duty for their country."

"But it's not. You said so yourself."

"You go when your country calls you. That's why I got shot up at Guadalcanal – because I love this country."

"I know you almost gave your life for your country, Mr. Hellman, and believe me, I respect that. But I love my country too. I just want it to do the right thing."

Larry felt a little guilty for having brought John's sons into the argument. After a pause, he said, "I know the one thing we agree on is that the real heroes are the ones who didn't come back."

They raised their mugs. "Here's to them."

"Hippie philosopher," John mumbled. "I gotta go."

JANET HAD SEEN the flyer on the wall:

U.S. Army Needs Nurses
Recruiter Here Friday 7 a.m. to 5 p.m.
Room 104 No Appointment Needed

Of course they needed nurses, with all the casualties over there. She had seen people at Shadyside with knife or gunshot wounds. It would be far worse in a war, with bombs and machine guns and God knows what else. She was a nurse – her profession was helping people – that's what she did in the hospital. It was a beautiful combination of knowledge, technology, and compassion, and she found it fulfilling. She was on the front lines, helping people in dire need of care. She loved her job. But where was the most need? Her conscience, her Catholic faith, and her parents had ingrained these ideals in her. Her father was a shining example in the way he had fought for his country, helped the youth of his neighborhood, and exhibited his patriotism. And after all, Florence Nightingale and Clara Barton, the iconic nurses, had become famous by tending to wounded soldiers in war. *Dad would be so proud!* "Don't get ahead of yourself, Janet," she said to herself. But it wouldn't hurt to talk with the recruiter.

Janet ended her shift at 4 and hurried to her 4:15 appointment with the Army recruiter. She walked into the room and met Lieutenant Paula Lofgren, a tall woman with Germanic features and short blonde hair, clad in an olive Army uniform that looked odd on a woman to Janet. Lieutenant

Lofgren stood and greeted her. "Please have a seat, Miss Hellman. So you are interested in joining the Army as a nurse?"

"Yes, I would like some information."

The Lieutenant smiled, discarding her initial formalism and warming to Janet. "What I can tell you is that we have a dire need. The wounded boys need you more than anyone. It's a job you will come to love. Many of our nurses re-enlist after their commitment, especially those in Vietnam. You provide care to those most in need, the most deserving. It is a chance to help your country by helping the brave wounded soldiers who protect all of us. Sometimes you help save them, sometimes you're the last face they see on this earth. I myself have held dying boys in my arms."

Janet was impressed. The Lieutenant was a paragon of compassionate competence, her eyes glistening as she spoke.

"Is it... dangerous?" Janet asked.

"It can be, but casualties among nurses are extremely rare. There is no guarantee in a combat zone, but we have the finest military in the world and it will provide protection. The soldiers love the nurses. 'Angels,' they call us."

"I am very interested."

"Why don't you take some information and look it over. It's a two-year enlistment with one full year in Vietnam. You would live in a tent and work in a hospital. It's hot there – with lots of bugs. But it's an adventure – and a mission. We save lives. The rates of survival are much higher now than in World War Two or Korea. That's partly due to technology but also due to the skill of our nurses."

She stood and handed Janet some pamphlets. They shook hands.

"Thank you very much," said Janet.

The Lieutenant looked her in the eye. "We need you. Our boys need you."

Janet was tingling all over. What a rewarding commitment this could be. As she drove home all she could think of was how proud Dad would be.

Janet parked her car and got out, carrying the Army pamphlets in one hand and her purse in the other. She was in her white nurse's uniform with white shoes. She smelled Dad's cigar. He was on the porch. He would be happy to see her, as he always was in his emotionally controlled way, with a sincere smile and "Hello Janet, how'd it go today?"

"Great, Daddy. I have something to show you. Wait till I change out of this uniform."

She walked into the house, in somewhat of a hurry. John watched her go. She was still the miracle he had never gotten over, even twenty-three years later. When he first saw that red little "bundle of joy," his life was changed – changed utterly. He recalled Gloria handing him Janet – not even a day old – and she clutched at him as he held her. It was his proudest moment, one he reminisced over many times. It brought him to tears for the first time in his adult life. That had not happened since that day, not even at his father's funeral. He had been blessed in life, with his marriage to Gloria and the later births of his sons, but with the birth of Janet – his first – he knew that God had saved him at Guadalcanal for that moment.

She came out to the porch in shorts and a polka dot top, carrying pamphlets. She was excited about something, which made John feel good. She had grown into a pretty young woman, with the light brown hair and expressive green eyes of her mother. Fortunately, John thought, she looked more like her mother than me. He put his cigar out, to better focus on something that was obviously important to her.

"What's up, Sweetheart?" John asked.

She had a big smile, like he remembered on her as a child giving him a Christmas present.

"Daddy... I met with the Army recruiter. I'm going to be a nurse – in Vietnam!"

She looked into his eyes, ready to embrace him, and saw... nothing. He was frozen, even scared-looking. His eyes didn't move, but filled with – tears? For a moment her nurse's mind thought he was having a stroke.

"Daddy... what's wrong?"

Her heart pounded with worry. She continued staring at him... no response. His mind seemed far away. After an agonizing wait, he blinked, and looked deeply into her eyes. He wasn't happy like she expected him to be. He struggled to speak. "Janet... Sweetheart... if I knew... that you were in harm's way..." He put his hand on hers.

Now his eyes overflowed, and tears ran down his cheeks. She had never seen this, even at Grandpa's funeral. It was unsettling. Again, he struggled. "If I knew... that you were in danger... halfway around the world... a little piece of me would die... every day..."

He had gotten it out, and couldn't speak any more. Janet was stunned. Her big tough Daddy looked so vulnerable, so scared.

"I thought you'd be so proud," she said softly. "I did it for you."

He couldn't stop the flow of tears. "Don't..." he managed to force out, and then couldn't continue. She hugged him, overwhelmed by his love. He hugged back. For a long time they were silent, embracing.

Her thoughts raced. *He'll adjust... he'll be proud. I need to do this.* They continued to hold each other. He felt so vulnerable to her, not moving, not speaking. She stood, and patted him on the back.

"I'll be safe. Our soldiers will keep me safe."

He did not react – no anger, no yelling, no laying down the law. He just looked so sad.

That night she saw her father, lying wounded on the beach in the Pacific. His face was contorted in agony. She heard his moans. She tried to get to him, but couldn't. She inched forward on the sand, struggling. She reached her arm toward him, but couldn't get to him. If only she could get to him... But she didn't have her stuff: no bandages, no scissors, no stethoscope. She woke up, looking around the room. She took a deep breath. It was just a dream.

She saw her father downstairs in his robe in the morning, drinking a cup of coffee. He said nothing. He looked sad, but accepting. He looked like he had aged overnight. She approached him slowly, and put her arm around his neck.

"I'm not going anywhere," she whispered. "I'm not going to Vietnam."

"Thank you," he said in a hoarse whisper. "Thank you."

A warm feeling came over her. At that moment Janet knew how much her father loved her. She would never again doubt that she was his pride and joy. She would make a life here - in Pittsburgh. But she would get her own place – just not in Vietnam. *Who wants to live in a tent with bugs anyway?*

THE END

BINDING FAITH

THE TRIPS TO visit his grandmother never failed to fascinate Patrick. He felt as if he were entering a different time, a slower-paced world. Her inner city neighborhood with its narrow, steep streets and tightly wedged houses was so different from the spacious, tree-lined street he lived on in Point Breeze. The main shopping district was right around the corner, with its smells of raw meat from the butcher shop, roasting peanuts in the Five and Ten Cent store, and tobacco from the cigar store. The old ladies with their big-handled shopping bags were in striking contrast to the stylish young women in Patrick's neighborhood. He loved the nostalgia Grandma's neighborhood evoked, and felt exhilarated by it. He recalled walking along the street as a child while holding his grandfather's hand. "Pap Pap" was a wonderfully entertaining man with a hearty laugh and a twinkle in his eye. He always had a big cigar that smelled good because it was *his* smell. Patrick still remembered him fondly, even though he had died ten years ago when Patrick was fifteen.

His grandmother was named Catherine Marie McNamara. She was his father's mother. She had two children and six grandchildren, including Patrick, the only child of her son Joseph. He had recently developed a close relationship with her that he would never have thought possible a few years ago. What a treasure she was! He had started to visit her by himself because he had had a renewal of religious feelings, and he knew that she was a good listener.

When he had gone away to college at Penn State, Patrick was happy to be freed from the bonds of Catholicism. He could sleep in and do as he pleased on Sunday, without having his parents watch over whether or not he went to church. He heard a lot of new ideas at the university, and struggled with the idea of whether or not there was a "God" who had created the universe. After about a year of intense, painful thought, he came to the conclusion that it was unknowable, and not that important anyway. He became a confirmed, indifferent agnostic. The only thing that really mattered was women and partying. Now, six years after graduating, he found that the struggle reawakened in his consciousness. He couldn't suppress the idea that there must be some idea for our being here, some "meaning" to life. Otherwise, why would anything exist at all?

His friends weren't concerned with such thoughts, and he found it difficult to talk with his parents about religion. The strident arguments of a few years ago about his lack of faith and refusal to attend church had extinguished any hope of communication there. Grandma, on the other hand, was forgiving and non-judgmental. She listened and encouraged Patrick, while not demanding anything. He had always thought of her as a pious, superstitious old Catholic, blindly following the ridiculous rituals of a primitive religion. These visits quickly demolished that idea. He discovered that she was well-versed in the philosophical ideas concerning the meaning of man's existence, and had read extensively in the field of religious philosophy. She explained to him many of the principal ideas of such luminaries as St. Augustine, St. Thomas Aquinas, G.K. Chesterton, and C.S. Lewis. All this from a woman with an eighth-grade education. Patrick, with his college degree, felt ignorant in comparison. Her faith was far more intellectual than he could have imagined. He was proud of his grandmother's depth of knowledge and intellectual prowess. This revelation had also taught him a valuable lesson about judging a person by external appearances.

Today he was going to take Grandma to church, and then to breakfast afterward. Entering her house was a further step into an older world. She had little religious statues and nicknacks everywhere. There was a distinct smell associated with her and her home, a peculiar, pleasant mixture of Lysol and "old lady" perfume. Everything was colorful and flowery, with soft reds, blues, and purples. White frill abounded.

"Good Morning, Patrick. God bless you."

"Good morning Grandma. Are you ready?"

"As ready as these legs can be, I guess."

It was difficult for her to negotiate the 24 steps that went directly from her front door to the sidewalk. Patrick privately winced as he held her arm for the slow, deliberate procession down the steps with her four-point walker. Osteoporosis had ravaged the bones in her legs so that walking was painful and difficult. Yet she still made the trip down the steps every day and still drove her little nine-year-old car. She was too strong-willed and stubborn to sit home and accept invalid status. This was another secret point of pride for Patrick. Her mind and spirit were as strong as her legs were weak.

St. Augustine's Church was only a few blocks away. It fit well with the neighborhood motif. Originally founded by German immigrants, it still retained the old world flavor. Inside, large statues beckoned with realistic eyes: the Blessed Mother in alluring blue, St. Joseph in warm brown, the Infant of Prague in a brilliant red coat. The altar area radiated gleaming gold and bright white linens. A life-sized crucifix hung on the center wall, showing a suffering Jesus with sad eyes, a crown of thorns, and blood dripping from his wounds. Incense was used unabashedly here, and a residual odor lingered permanently. This was a real Catholic church. The modern-style church Patrick's family belonged to seemed sterile by comparison, with its stark, minimalist structure and ample parking lot. He was beginning to understand the power and beauty of Catholic sensuality and ritual through his association with Grandma. It evoked a bone-deep awareness of the presence of God in the world.

CATHERINE FELT TRULY blessed by this late-blooming relationship with her grandson Patrick. She had always felt a special affinity for him. He was such a sensitive, introspective boy, so unlike her other grandchildren. She had been kept informed about his crisis of faith, and had prayed hard for him to see the light. She had watched her hot-tempered son Joe react by badgering and threatening Patrick, driving him farther away. Finally she felt compelled to step in and order Joe to stop it, as she feared Patrick would become embittered beyond hope. Joe obeyed, as he usually did, and Patrick was left alone.

Now, as she neared death, Catherine saw the beginning fruits of her careful orchestration and heartfelt prayer. She saw the seeds of faith sprouting in Patrick, and felt a deep gratitude to God. He was still a young male, however, wild and free and beautiful. He liked to drink and carouse with his buddies, like most of the young men she had seen in her long life. She felt sure that his intelligence and sensitivity would steer him through this dangerous period to eventually settle down with a nice girl. She would pray him through it in the time she had left. For now, she was thrilled that he confided so much in her, a living relic past her prime.

At first Patrick thought it peculiar that Grandma liked to talk about her own death. At 85, with osteoporotic legs, she felt she had lived long enough and was ready to meet her Maker. She truly saw death as a mere step from a temporary physical world to a different, more permanent spiritual world. As such, it was certainly not something to fear. She was very Irish in that way. She recounted strange Irish funeral traditions from the old country, which shocked Patrick for their calloused attitude toward death. Often the corpse was brought to the wake and seated at a table, while the raucous "mourners" threw drinks down its gullet.

Grandma casually talked of her own funeral arrangements and of how she wanted her funeral to be a beautiful experience for the family. She wanted Patrick to read from Paul's letter to the Corinthians with its rebuke "O Death, where is thy sting?" She knew which hymns she wanted sung at the Mass, and had commissioned Patrick to make sure that they were indeed sung. They were all traditional ones like "Ave Maria" and "Jesus My Lord." Patrick had lobbied hard for "On Eagles' Wings," a newer one that he thought would be a nice, upbeat conclusion. Grandma, however, declared that her funeral Mass would conclude with "Holy God We Praise Thy Name," a dramatic, traditional hymn. Apparently she had planned this for a long time, and was not going to change it. She also wanted Patrick to sprinkle her precious holy water from Lourdes on her casket at the end of the ceremony. This would be their special farewell.

Patrick had discovered that he could talk with Grandma about girls, always a mysterious, troubling subject. He couldn't even begin to discuss this with his parents, and his good-time friends offered little useful advice. They spoke only of conquests, topping each other's stories with bold exaggeration. Grandma seemed to understand the basics of relationships. She understood girls and Patrick. She gave good, practical advice and was more help than he could get anywhere else. He could pour out his soul to her about his hopes and dreams for a continuing series of young women. She lent a sympathetic ear. Patrick knew she wouldn't live much longer, and he knew he would miss her.

THE MONDAY MORNING funeral Mass was a somber affair. It was not at all like Catherine's description of the hopeful Irish funeral buoyed by the idea that death is not the end. Patrick's mother and father were almost numb with grief. The traditional "Ave Maria" and "Jesus My Lord" were sung, and the upbeat "On Eagles' Wings" at the end did little to inject hope into an overpoweringly sad ceremony. Prayers were read at the grave before a listless, despairing assembly of family and friends. But the saddest sight of all occurred at the end of the graveside ceremony. A bent, feeble old woman slowly and painfully made her way to the edge of the grave, with two strong men on either side to aid her, and a four-point walker clutched in her right hand. Her ancient face was deeply lined with the grief of a thousand years. The mourners watched as she sprinkled holy water on the casket that bore the body of her grandson, Patrick McNamara.

THE END

A GIFT FOR SARAH

DEAN COULD SEE the road getting slicker as he drove out Route 30 toward Westmoreland Mall. It would be much worse in the mountains to the east. Thank God he didn't have to go there today. An early December snowstorm was expected to drop two or three inches over the Pittsburgh area this afternoon. His old Honda Accord was dependable, but it would be nice to have a big four-wheel-drive vehicle that was immune to snow and could carry more of his samples. *Maybe some day.* He sold gift items to retail stores, mainly card shops and gift shops. The Christmas rush was just about over now. The store owners bought their Christmas items in October and November. Some bought a little more during the first week of December, as they evaluated early Christmas season results.

It hadn't been a good year. Consumer confidence was down, and Dean's sales were down slightly from last year. His boss was not pleased. The man didn't care that there was a recession – he wanted more sales. And he accepted no excuses.

Dean had done well in his first four years as a salesman. He had built good relationships with the store owners in his territory, and increased his sales every year. The job was challenging and stimulating. The store owners could be tough and insensitive – they were aggressive people trying to succeed in a competitive business – and Dean had to be well-prepared and aggressive himself. But he never regretted leaving his dead-end government job five years ago. His potential earnings were unlimited. He was much happier now.

This year, his fifth, had been difficult. A recession with massive job losses had kept consumer spending down. "Corporate down-sizing" they called it. What a euphemism! Dean's meteoric rise in the first four years had hit a brick wall. The boss was furious. *But what can you do?* Dean thought. *It's certainly not for lack of effort.*

The only "boss" Dean really cared about was his daughter Sarah. He kept her picture on the dashboard to remind him of why he was working. He had a son now also, Sean Matthew, just three months old. But the picture of Sarah on the dashboard had driven his success. Many times he had stared at it just before going in to make a sale. It calmed him, it stimulated him, it prepared him to do his best, just like a boxer preparing himself in the corner before a big fight.

Sarah was seven years old now, but the picture was of her as a three-year-old. It was a time Dean fondly remembered, Daddy's little girl who was so dependent on him. They were still close, but she was starting to develop some independence now. She had friends, school, dancing, and sports activities. He wasn't the center of her world any more. The picture reminded him of that precious time, of the little girl he would always carry in his heart.

HE PULLED INTO the parking lot of Westmoreland Mall. He had an appointment with Karen Parker, owner of Karen's Gift Shop. She was one of the nicest owners in his territory. He packed up his samples and took a long look at Sarah's picture. A good sale here would make an impression on the boss. *Late season, second-effort Dean.*

He walked through the mall, which was beautifully decorated for Christmas. Red Santas, green holly, white snowmen, fluffy-cotton snow, majestic reindeer – it was all there. *Everything but Baby Jesus.* Dean went first to the men's room to groom himself. Appearance was important in this business. *You don't take anything for granted. Neat hair, neat tie, shiny shoes – look good. Stand up straight – act confident – be friendly – smile.* His overcoat was getting old. It was a little frayed at the edges. But this would be its last Christmas season. His wife Kathleen had put a beautiful new wool coat on layaway for his Christmas present. It would strain their budget, but she considered it an investment. He would hit the road in January with an impressive new appearance, setting records as he sold tons of gift items for Valentine's Day, St. Patrick's Day, Easter, and Spring.

Dean sometimes wondered if he were stuck in a time warp. His coat, his car, and the picture of Sarah had been bought at the same time. All three were getting older, and would have to be replaced. The coat would be the first step out of his rut.

HE WALKED INTO a busy little gift shop. Karen's sales clerk was ringing up an order, and several customers were browsing the merchandise.

"Hi Dean!" the clerk shouted.

She was a pretty blonde, and it was nice to get a friendly reaction from her. He made a point of remembering names. It was best to be on good terms with everyone,

"Hi Lisa! How's it going?"

"Oh, we're pretty busy. Go ahead into the office. Karen's expecting you."

"Thanks."

He walked back to the office and looked in. Karen was writing furiously. She looked up.

"Oh, Dean! Come on in. What do you have for me?"

He showed her the items she had requested, and a few others he had brought along just in case.

"How's business?" he asked.

"Oh, not too bad. A little down from last year, but really not too bad under the circumstances."

He laughed. "Good. That's about my situation too."

Karen was the type of woman Dean liked. She was smart and could be tough, but she had a heart. She always treated him with respect and kindness. She was an attractive woman in her late forties – slim, pretty, and immaculately groomed. Long auburn curls framed a face dominated by lively, intelligent eyes. She had built a successful business by herself since her divorce years ago.

"How's the new baby?" she asked.

Dean beamed with pride. "Oh, just great. He's getting bigger every day."

"Sean Matthew, right?"

"Yes, Sean Matthew."

"And Sarah and Kathleen?"

"Great, just great."

"I'll bet Sarah's really looking forward to Christmas this year."

"You got that right. I think this is her last year for Santa, though. She's getting older, you know."

She noticed sadness in his voice.

"Aren't we all?"

They both laughed.

"So what do you have for me, Dean? The pins and music boxes?"

"Yeah, and a few others." She looked them over.

"Okay, I'll take a hundred of each of the holly and tree pins, and ten of each music box type."

Dean made his pitch. "You sure that's all? I also have these sleighs and snowmen. They could sell beyond Christmas – you know, winter things."

She paused.

"Okay, fifteen of each music box type and two dozen of those 'winter things.'"

Dean smiled in appreciation as he wrote up the order.

"I'll have these here by Friday – Federal Express. And thank you."

She stood up and offered her hand.

"You're quite welcome. And have a wonderful Christmas."

"I will, Karen. Merry Christmas to you too."

"You know, they do grow up, Dean. She's not a baby anymore." She paused. "But when they turn out to be nice adults it's the most rewarding thing in the world."

"Thanks – thanks Karen. I'll see you next month. Valentine's Day's coming up."

"That's right. See you then."

DEAN PULLED THE car into the garage next to the little rented house where he and his family lived. Some day they would own a nice big house with lots of land. It felt good to be home. The roads were getting bad as the snow continued.

He walked in as Kathleen was nursing the baby. She looked up and smiled warmly.

"Hi Honey! How'd it go?"

"Pretty good. Karen Parker took some extra merchandise. How's things on the home front?"

She nodded toward the suckling baby.

"This little guy has quite an appetite. He eats a lot more than Sarah ever did."

Dean rubbed his finger over Sean Matthew's cheek.

"Hey Buddy!"

The baby kept sucking vigorously while Kathleen spoke.

"I got Sarah's keyboard today. It's hidden with the rest of the presents in the basement. It's very nice. She'll like it. It was about two hundred dollars."

"Is that what she asked for?" Dean interrupted.

"Well, she'll need it when she starts taking piano lessons after the holidays. She keeps talking about that porcelain doll she saw at Macy's, but we can't afford that."

"Why not?" he asked weakly.

"Honey, it's three hundred and fifty dollars! We've already spent too much for Christmas, and we're not exactly rolling in dough this year."

"I know, but if that's what she wants…"

"Don't be silly. We can't afford it. Shhh."

Sarah and her friend Ashley breezed through the living room.

"Hi Daddy!"

They ran upstairs to Sarah's room.

MONEY WAS A difficult subject for Dean. He had promised Kathleen that he would provide enough income so that she could have children and not have to work. They had two children and she was still a full-time mother, but they were struggling. They could not afford to buy a home or the bigger vehicle he needed for his job and for family activities. He loved Kathleen deeply, and wanted to keep his promise.

Dean felt that Kathleen was a miracle in his life. Before her he had been so unfocused and disorganized, a playboy bouncing from girl to girl. Kathleen was the first one to stand up to him, to make demands on him. He was first attracted to her looks, but then was drawn to her in a deeper way by her assertive personality. She was, in contrast to himself, focused, organized, and disciplined. She knew what she wanted, and she wanted him to be a part of it. She was also devoutly Catholic, which pleased his parents. She had patiently brought him back to the Church, for which he was now grateful.

Kathleen was tall and willowy, with wavy, honey-brown hair, full red lips, and luscious healthy skin. But what Dean liked most about her was her big blue eyes with long eyelashes. She could express a wide range of emotions just by flickering her eyes. Her face was the essence of beauty, and he never tired of it. In fact, it grew on him more and more. It was a wonderful thing to wake up to in the morning. She was having a little trouble shedding weight after the second birth, but he knew that she had the discipline to do it eventually. She looked so warm and content when she nursed Sean Matthew.

SARAH AND ASHLEY were walking down the hill on their way home from school. Sarah, the taller one, had wavy blonde hair that brushed the shoulders of her red cloth coat. Ashley's reddish-brown curls spilled over the collar of her blue ski jacket. Both had cute little pixie faces. They had just finished the last day of school until after New Year's. Christmas was only five days away, and they were both excited.

"What did you tell Santa, Ashley?"

"I told him I wanted My Size Barbie…"

"I told him I wanted a bee-yoo-tiful baby doll I saw at Macy's," Sarah panted. "Ooh, I can't wait."

Behind them strode Megan McDonald, ten years old and appropriately condescending to the mere seven-year-olds in front of her.

"You guys don't still believe in Santa Claus, do you?" she interrupted.

"What do you mean?" asked Sarah.

"Do you really think that one guy can deliver millions of toys over the whole world in one night?"

They looked at each other.

"Then who does it?" Sarah asked.

"It's your Dad, stupid, who do you think?" Megan laughed.

"My Dad?"

"Yes! Your Dad brings your presents. Santa Claus is your Dad!"

She strode off triumphantly.

ON SATURDAY DEAN took Sarah with him to buy a live Christmas tree. She was quiet. Was something on her mind? She "helped" him drag the tree in to the stand in the living room. He and Sarah would decorate it and surprise Kathleen, who had taken Sean Matthew to the doctor for his checkup. Kathleen and Dean had arranged this so that he and Sarah could "surprise" her with a fully decorated tree when she came home. Sarah loved surprising her Mom.

Dean pulled out the boxes of garlands, ornaments, and lights. He noticed that Sarah was not as excited about this as in prior years. She had her mother's expressive eyes, and he could tell that she was still deep in thought. She looked at him, the blue eyes very serious.

"Daddy, how does Santa Claus deliver toys to all the kids in the world in just one night?"

Oh God! My baby! Dean chose his words carefully.

"Well, he probably has helpers. Yeah… that's how he does it."

She frowned. "You mean the real Santa doesn't visit everyone's house?"

Please God. Just one more year.

"Well, I guess not. But he makes sure everything gets there."

"But do they ever get it wrong?"

"Oh, I don't think so. No, they never get it wrong."

The baby blues blinked and stared. He could tell that she wasn't quite convinced.

KATHLEEN AND THE baby burst through the door.

"Oh my God! What a beautiful tree!"

Sarah squealed with delight.

"We did it! Daddy and me did it!"

Kathleen hugged Sarah. "It is so beautiful! What a surprise!"

Sarah clapped her hands together and smiled from ear to ear. Her blue eyes lit up the room. Dean felt relieved. He hoped that she had forgotten about Santa's logistical problems, at least until after Christmas.

THE KIDS WERE in bed, and Dean and Kathleen had some time to themselves, as long as Sean Matthew didn't wake up. Christmas was only a few days away. Everything was done but the baking. Dean would be home until after New Year's. The retailers had no time to buy his goods now. One of the aspects of his job that he liked best was the long Christmas vacation. From the middle of December until early January he was off. He could help decorate and prepare for Christmas. He was disturbed this evening, though, and needed to talk with Kathleen.

"Honey, I think we need to get that porcelain doll."

"Oh, no, Dean. Sarah will have plenty of presents. She doesn't need any more. And you know we can't afford it."

"But it's what she wants. Maybe we can take back the keyboard."

Kathleen frowned.

"The doll costs a lot more than the keyboard. We can't give her everything. Do you want to spoil her?"

"I want her to be happy on Christmas morning."

"She'll be happy on Christmas morning. She'll have a ton of presents."

"But she asked for the doll."

The blue eyes flickered. She was getting annoyed at his persistence.

"We can't afford the doll, and a lot of other things we need."

His cheeks reddened.

"It's not my fault there's a recession," he said, his voice getting louder.

"Well, it's not mine either," she snapped back.

"I'll take my coat back..."

"No! That coat is important for our future! A lot more important than some silly overpriced baby doll!"

They stared at each other, half angry, half apologetic. Sean Matthew's cry pierced the awkward silence.

"See, you made me wake the baby up," Kathleen mumbled as she started toward the stairs.

A pair of little feet scampered across the upstairs hallway and back into bed.

They argued several more times about the doll. Dean just wouldn't let it die. Finally he took the initiative and bought it, trading in the new coat that was on layaway. They were about the same price, so their tight budget was intact. When he told Kathleen, she shook her head in disgust at his short-sightedness, but didn't fight him on it. She was tired of the argument. Sarah would have her porcelain doll on Christmas morning.

When the big day finally dawned, Sarah was up early, urging Dean and Kathleen to wake up. Kathleen got Sean Matthew up, and they all went downstairs together.

Under the tree stood the doll, with its white porcelain skin and red satin dress. Real blonde hair framed its delicately featured face. Its bright green eyes beckoned through the dim light of dawn. Sarah ran to it, breathless, hugging it and showing it to both of them repeatedly. She ignored her other presents. Even Kathleen was touched. Dean was relieved and happy. Everything had worked out. Kathleen was such a good sport about it, even though she had been right. He couldn't imagine loving her any more than he did now.

It was time to go to church. Dean would take Sarah to the early Mass, while Kathleen stayed home with Sean Matthew. Kathleen would go by herself to a later Mass.

Dean and Sarah walked up the hill to St. Bede's, holding hands. They stopped at the manger before going into the church. They looked at the statues of Joseph, Mary, and Baby Jesus, along with shepherds, lambs, a camel, and the Three Wise Men. Real straw was strewn about the floor. Sarah waited until they were the only ones in the manger. She tugged at his coat.

"Daddy…"

"What, Honey?"

He had never seen her look so serious. The big blue eyes were wide open.

"Daddy… I know that there's no Santa Claus."

Jesus, Mary, and Joseph!

Dean just stood there, dumbfounded.

"I know it was you who brought my baby doll. Oh, Daddy, I love you so much!"

She embraced him around his waist and squeezed as hard as her little arms could squeeze. He fought back the tears, hugging her back.

"I love you too, baby."

DEAN'S HEART WAS soaring as they walked into the church, holding hands. *What a beautiful Christmas morning!* In the vestibule he could see himself and Sarah reflected in the glass windows that enclosed the church bulletin board. He stopped, stood straight and tall, and smiled. The old coat never looked better.

THE END

CLEAR VISION

"SOME DECISIONS ARE too important to be made sober," declared Brian Burke to anyone at the bar within earshot. "I see things much more clearly when I'm drunk." He took a long swig from his High Life bottle, and a quick puff on his cigarette. He was nearing retirement, and trying to decide when to go. He had pretty much decided – he would go at age 66 when he had his 40 years in. That was still almost two years away. He was comfortable in his seat at Dave's Café – *his* seat to all the regulars. He liked making ironic statements about drinking, but he was dead serious about seeing things more clearly under the influence of alcohol. The other regulars found him entertaining. His easygoing manner and all out endorsement of drinking made them more comfortable in their habit. He liked the philosophy of the ancient Persians (or was it a Greek city-state?) that an important issue must be debated twice: once in a sober state, and once under the influence of alcohol to get a full perspective. He wasn't sure why they bothered with the sober part.

Brian's family members and co-workers told him he had a drinking problem, and some encouraged him to try AA meetings. He went once to appease them, and thought it was all bullshit. He didn't want to stop. He liked getting drunk. He knew how to handle it. He took aspirin and drank a full glass of water before going to bed. He mostly kept his drinking to Friday and Saturday nights, so as not to miss work. He had been a good employee as a welfare caseworker for the Commonwealth of Pennsylvania for 38 years, and knew his job well. He was never a violent drunk. In fact, drinking made him even more friendly and sociable.

His drinking was not without problems. He knew he could never have "a beer or two." Once he started drinking he kept going until he was good and drunk. His wife had left him years ago because of it. He didn't understand why. He had a good career and between his job and hers as a secretary, they had a good, steady income. He was a good father to his two children. So what if he got drunk? He had never cheated on her or hit her. He was kind and supportive. She knew from the start that he drank. Why did she leave after 18 years? It was something they could never see eye-to-eye on.

Even after the divorce, he contributed to raising the kids, Brian Junior and Julie. He paid for their college tuition at great sacrifice to himself. He still owed money for it. They both became pharmacists, and made good money. He had a good relationship with both. Brian gave him free Viagra samples for his off-and-on girlfriends (drinking partners, more accurately.) He was too embarrassed to ask Julie for Viagra. She was forever trying to convince him to try anti-alcohol or anti-nicotine drugs, to no avail. This Saturday night Dave's Café was full with regulars and a few others, mostly from the local Point Breeze neighborhood. Brian had known some since grade school at St. Bede. It was a good place to get a sandwich and a beer, watch sports on TV, and engage in male conversation. Brian drank his High Life and smoked, rarely eating unless it was at the end of the night to sober up. He usually stayed until well after midnight, downing ten beers or more and a shot of Irish whiskey, but who's counting? No one else drank High Life. Gene the bartender ordered it just for Brian, who had been drinking it for years. Some of the patrons were sons of guys he had grown up with. The young guys liked him. His enjoyment of drinking was contagious, and assuaged the guilt some may have felt.

"I see it now," he said. "Full retirement, Social Security… I'll be making more than I am working."

He had it all figured out, to the penny. "When I retire, every night's Friday night and every morning's Saturday morning. I can get drunk every night and not have to worry." It would be like he died and went to heaven. He dreamed of it often. No work hassles, doing whatever he wanted. It was coming up fast. Retirement…

"You'll have it made," said Gene, who opened him another High Life. The Pirate game was on the TV.

Brian pontificated in his endearing way. "Y'know, the best baseball players were alcoholics. Babe Ruth, Jimmy Foxx, Mickey Mantle… all drunks. These guys today with their steroids ruined baseball. Gimme the old drunks any day."

Brian had been a high school and college baseball player, and had a reverence for the game. They called him the "Irish Assassin," not for anything to do with guns or fighting, but because as a catcher he gunned down runners attempting to steal bases with his strong, accurate arm.

The door burst open and in walked a huge man. Paul Crissman was a shade under six feet tall, and weighed well over 300 pounds. He had a full, bushy salt-and-pepper beard with long, shaggy, mostly gray hair. Everything about Paul was big – head, hands, arms, legs, shoulders. He was remarkably spry and energetic for a man that size in his sixties. He saw Brian and embraced him in a true "bear" hug. "My man! The Assassin!" boomed Paul's loud, deep voice, the kind common in men with huge chest cavities. Brian slipped off the chair, losing his balance in his drunken state. Embarassed, he said, "Sorry, Paul, I'm drunk."

"Never apologize for being drunk," boomed Paul. "Don't you never apologize for being drunk. Gimme an Iron, and another ... what's that shit you drink?"

"High Life."

"A High Life for the Irish Assassin."

Brian toasted Paul. "To the hero of the sixty-seven championship game."

Paul laughed. "That was forty-some years ago. Most of these people in here weren't even born then."

"I don't give a shit," Brian argued. "It was the greatest game in City League history. They should know."

Most of the guys in the bar knew that Paul had been some kind of football hero from days gone by. He certainly looked the part. Brian decided to recount the details for them. Paul's presence always made him more animated and talkative.

"It was 1967. Allderdice had a great team that year for the first time ever. We played Westinghouse, who was always tough. They'd won something like nineteen outta the last twenty championships under Pete

Dimperio. Both teams were undefeated, ripping the shit out of every other team. So they met for the city championship at South Stadium. And Paul here was the best lineman in the city, both offense and defense. He was two hundred and seventy pounds in high school, which in those days was huge. And he could move.

"Now I gotta set the scene. That was a time of big racial tension... riots in Homewood and the Hill, big social upheaval going on. Westinghouse was all black, Allderdice was all white. So you have two great undefeated teams, white against black, the whole city riveted. The game went back and forth. At the end Allderdice had a twenty to thirteen lead. Westinghouse had the ball first and goal on our one yard line with under a minute to play. It looked like a tie was imminent."

Brian paused to catch his breath, his eyes alive, his hands animated, even holding his beer bottle.

"Well, Westinghouse ran the ball three times. Paul stopped them all three times at the line of scrimmage. It came down to the final play, fourth and one, seconds to go. They give the ball to their best running back – quick as hell."

He paused for dramatic effect.

"Paul smashes through their line, grabs the kid in the backfield, and throws him to the ground – game over."

Brian could feel his heart pounding as he spoke. He had been there, a backup linebacker who rarely played, but Paul's best buddy since early grade school. He thought he saw a tear trickle down Paul's hairy cheek.

"The fights! The riots after that game! We got the worst of that, but we were the champs. Thanks to my good buddy Paul here."

"All right, enough of that ancient history shit," said Paul.

Brian had an audience now, and couldn't stop talking.

"One more history fact," he said. "You know, when people told Lincoln that Grant was a drunk, do you know what he said?"

Several at the bar groaned. They had heard Brian tell this one many times. Brian didn't care. He liked it so much he told it almost every night.

"Lincoln said, 'Find out what he's drinking and give it to my other generals.' "

Brian laughed at his own story and raised his bottle. "To Ulysses S. Grant. A man after my own heart."

After a few more beers, Paul rose to say good-bye. "I have to drive out to O'Hara Township, not like yinz guys still in the Breeze."

He hugged Brian and whispered in his ear, "Thanks for the stories, buddy." He set Brian on the barstool gently and walked out.

"That's a helluva football player, and a helluva man," Brian announced.

He said to the bartender, "Time to eat, Gene. Gimme that big cheeseburger with the bacon, mustard, and onions. And some fries. And some coffee to keep me awake for the drive home."

Brian knew he needed to sober up before driving this time. He sipped the coffee, and then Gene brought out the food. Brian started wolfing it down. It was a big, juicy hamburger, greasy and tasty. It tasted good.

"I can feel that grease draining the alcohol right out of my blood."

He finished the burger, and felt good... a little mellow. He paid his tab, and got down from his bar stool. He could stand and balance himself fine. He was a catcher, after all.

"Be careful, Brian. You OK?" Gene yelled.

"I'm good," he answered. "I'm calling it a night. Have a good one!"

He walked without difficulty out to the sidewalk, and the night breeze refreshed him. His car wasn't in its usual spot. He had had to park a block and a half away, an uphill trek. He started up the hill. He felt a little short of breath, and a little dizzy. He stopped to get his bearings. *It's that big cheeseburger. How many beers did I have?* He chuckled. *Who's counting?*

He continued up the hill. He felt something grab his chest, deep inside, squeezing him. He couldn't get his breath, and sunk to his knees. No one was around. He toppled over, his face brushing the sidewalk. But he could see it all with clear vision. The little twigs and clumps of grass at the sidewalk cracks by his face were part of God's creation, as was he. He had taken care of his kids, tried to do his best. He loved them, and they loved him. He wasn't such a bad guy at all. He needed to make it to retirement, now less than two years... if only he could move. He couldn't even make it to his car... or even to his feet. It felt like a ton of bricks on his chest, or maybe Paul Crissman. He wasn't scared. He could even joke about it. *Paul, get off my chest!* The alcohol made him so mellow, even content. He could see everything clearly in his mind, if only he... could... breathe. *Jesus... help me...*

THE END

RITE OF PASSAGE

A MEMOIR

THE DREADED NEWS had come. I was scheduled to serve the Holy Terror, Father Enright. It was a big step for a young altar boy. Serving the kindly assistant pastor, Father Staab, was a pleasant experience that made me feel increasingly competent on the altar, and closer to God. He taught us the beautiful Latin prayers, the proper reverence, and when and how to make the right moves. The younger altar boys like me served only Father Staab. One had to be an experienced veteran to serve Father Enright. My time had come.

The Reverend John F. Enright ("Himself" to my mother) had founded St. Bede parish in the 1920s in the Point Breeze section of Pittsburgh. By the 1950s when my family moved to the neighborhood from Lawrenceville, it was bursting with kids. Families of ten, eleven, or even thirteen children were not unusual. We had nine, slightly above average. The parish was mostly Irish, with Germans and Italians also well-represented. Most of the very large families were Irish.

A new church had been constructed in 1950. It was a modern-looking gray stone building, unlike the Gothic, steeple-dominated churches typical of Pittsburgh's inner city. A statue of Bede the Venerable was embedded above the front doors. School and church buildings were connected, symbolizing Himself's tight control over both.

But the modern appearance was deceiving. It was 1960, and the liberalizing changes of Vatican II were still a few years away. In Father Enright's little fiefdom, it may as well have been 1560.

He was in his early eighties, and the words grouchy, crabby, belligerent – even miserable – were used to describe him by those who supported and respected him. Others thought much worse of him. Most thought he was that way because of his age, but my mother maintained that he had always been miserable.

He had abundant white hair, and soft, pinkish, gently wrinkled skin that resembled a Lady Finger pastry. He wore little wire-rimmed glasses that hung on a pugnacious nose softened by age. He had vivid, darting eyes that were always searching for somebody doing something wrong. He had a huge, protruding belly that stretched out his cassock like he was eight months pregnant. He needed a cane to walk due to his weight and arthritis. His ancient voice roared with authority. It seemed louder than it actually was, because when he spoke everyone was so, so quiet.

He was the strict, hard-headed Irish pastor of yore who ran his parish with an iron hand. To describe him as "old-fashioned" or "pre-Vatican II" would not do him justice. He was "pre-Genesis" if he was anything. The beleaguered assistant priests who worked under him struggled to make the best of a difficult situation. Father Staab, and later, Father Dompka, made courageous efforts behind his back to establish athletic teams and a parish bulletin. To this day his former assistants regale their colleagues with Father Enright stories at priestly gatherings. The stories need no exaggeration.

THE SYMPATHETIC LOOKS from my classmates only increased my fear. I had an impending date with a legendary tyrant. When you're ten years old and frightened, there's only one thing to do – run home and tell Mom.

By 1960 my perpetually pregnant mother had had eight of her nine children: all single births, all about a year-and-a-half apart. I was second, and the oldest boy. She could handle any crisis. She would know what to tell me.

She looked upon Father Enright with mocking bemusement, dubbing him with the mildly irreverent title of "Himself." But she didn't have to serve him. She only had to watch him from the pews.

I blurted out the news: "Mom, I'm scheduled to serve Father Enright in three weeks."

She understood my apprehension, and tried to soothe me with Irish fatalism.

"Don't worry about it now. He's a very old man. He could be dead by then."

We both knew it wasn't going to happen, but the hope would sustain me for now.

THREE WEEKS LATER he was still alive, and I got up to serve the 8:00 Mass. There were some special features for a Father Enright Mass. He had his own small altar off to the side of the main one due to limited mobility. He had his own giant cruets (water and wine vessels) and he said all of the altar boys' responses himself to speed things up. The entire Mass lasted about 15 minutes, less than half the normal time span.

Fortunately I would be serving with John Hurley, two years older than me, who was the only altar boy that Father Enright liked. As I nervously fixed my cassock and surplice in the altar boys' sacristy, John gave me a few precautionary instructions.

"Pour all of the wine into the chalice, and one tiny drop of water. And don't get too far ahead when we march out to the altar." He knew it was my first time with Father Enright, and was trying to put me at ease before he left to help Father Enright put on his vestments. I finished dressing and said a heartfelt Hail Mary. Then I crossed the hallway to meet Himself.

I opened the door to the priests' sacristy and timidly walked in. Himself was sitting in a chair against the wall facing me, about five feet away in the cramped quarters. I nodded with all the respect I could muster and said, "Good Morning, Father." He just stared at me angrily with pursed lips. I had no idea what I had done wrong, if anything, until he boomed "Close the door!" Of course I closed it quickly and quietly. I was off to a bad start.

John had filled the cruets with wine and water. (They were at least twice as big as Father Staab's.) I was sent out to the altar to light the candles. All preparations were completed, and we were ready to go.

John held Father Enright by the right arm (he could not walk without the support) and I walked to his left. The procession out to his altar was a tricky maneuver. We had to exit the sacristy and swing right about 270 degrees, with one altar boy holding up an enormous, slow-moving priest, and the other marching on his left flank, trying to keep a perfect line. The entire trip was only about twenty feet, but it took several minutes to complete. I was careful to stay in perfect alignment as we kept turning right.

At about the halfway point, I must have gotten all of three or four inches ahead of where I was supposed to be, for he stopped, stared right through me, and bellowed for the entire church to hear: "Send me a postcard when you get there!" I was now completely humiliated as we completed the arc and delivered Himself to his altar.

The Mass went smoothly enough and very quickly. He whipped through the prayers with astonishing speed. We gave no response, not even the traditional Suscipiat bow. We just knelt and listened to a master crafts-man. At the Offertory I remembered the special instructions. While most priests mixed water and wine about equally, Himself liked a lot of wine and one drop of water. I dutifully poured the huge container of wine into his chalice. The single drop of water I added must have been a little large, for he roughly clanked the edge of his chalice against my water cruet to protest the dilution of his wine. Later, when I gave him the towel to wipe his hands, he threw it on the floor at my feet instead of handing it back to me. The second time I gave him the towel, near the end of Mass, he wiped his hands and just dropped it – I was making progress. We completed the Mass and marched back to the sacristy in a perfect line. I had survived the first day.

I SERVED HIM many times in the next few years. I had passed the critical test for altar boys in our parish, and could now counsel younger boys about the perils of serving Father Enright. For generations of boys at St. Bede, he represented an important step in growing up. If you could serve Father Enright, you could handle anything.

Father Enright died in January, 1968, a few days short of his 89th birthday. The only remaining trace of him at St. Bede is a plaque with a flat bust of his head in the vestibule. No longer does his booming voice rattle the walls. No longer are giant cruets carried out to a compact altar on the left. His tyrannical style, too, is long gone. His ways died with him. May he, and they, rest in peace.

THE END

CARL'S CREW

ON A JUNE Monday in 1967 I started my first job, as a summer laborer at Homewood Cemetery. I didn't know what to expect. I had never had a real job before. I had gone with my mother to an office downtown to get a "work permit," since I was under eighteen. I would turn seventeen in July. The edge of the cemetery was across the street from my house. I could walk to the main entrance in less than five minutes.

I reported to the shed at the gate near Forbes and Dallas avenues at 8 a.m. to Bud Wilson, who was the foreman. He had me fill out some papers, and then introduced me to the crew. He said that "Carl" would be in charge and would show me what to do. Carl was an energetic, friendly nineteen-year-old. He wore jeans and a white tee shirt with very short sleeves, revealing muscular upper arms. He had thick glasses and a big smile with lots of teeth. He seemed happy and easy to get along with. We boarded the truck, which had a big flatbed with wooden sides and a back that folded down into a ramp. The other guys wheeled the grass cutting machines onto the truck. The crew included Bing, Speedy, Bill, Carl, and me. Buddy drove. Carl sat next to me. Bill was a summer employee like me, but had started a few weeks earlier. Bing appeared to be in his forties. He was round-shouldered and heavy through the middle. He seemed to be leaning forward all the time. He wore a light blue shirt with buttons and a collar, and brown cuffed work pants. He wore dark shoes. The rest of us wore tee shirts, jeans, and sneakers. He had a baseball cap with a long bill pulled down low over his face, with no lettering on it. He had a goofy look on his face and didn't seem to notice me. I wondered if he was "not right." Speedy appeared to be in his late forties at least. He was short with a sturdy chest and shoulders. He was bald on top, and had short graying hair around the sides. His jaw jutted forward. He was unshaven – or poorly shaven – with salt and pepper whiskers all over his chin and cheeks. About every ten seconds his head jerked violently. He looked vigilant and well aware of his surroundings, unlike Bing, who appeared to be in a stupor. Bill seemed to be a nice kid, with an open, honest face. He was tall, lean, and tan, with short dark hair.

We bounced along on the paved cemetery road through the grave-stones and well-kept grass, headed for the area that we were assigned to cut that day. I would be cutting grass with the rest of the crew – Carl's crew. We rode quietly up and down the hills until suddenly Bing and Speedy stood up. Bing doffed his cap, revealing a full head of straight brown oily hair. They broke into song together, hands across hearts.

Hail to Pitt! Hail to Pitt! Every loyal son!

Hail to Pitt! Hail to Pitt! Till the victory's won!

Rah! Rah! Rah!

Both were tone deaf. Carl, rolling with laughter, explained to me that we had just passed the grave of Jock Sutherland, the renowned Pitt foot-ball coach.

Homewood Cemetery was 200 acres of rolling green hills in the East End of Pittsburgh. It had a large stone English Tudor-Gothic chapel, wrought-iron gates and fencing, and a picturesque spring-fed pond. It con-tained scores of beautiful mausoleums, many of which housed the remains of tycoons of Pittsburgh industry, such as Henry Clay Frick, H.J. Heinz, Michael Benedum, and several Mellons. It had a Greek section with Greek crosses and script, and a Chinese section with Chinese characters engraved on the tombstones. Sometimes family members left food for their departed loved ones at the Chinese graves. It even had a "colored section," de facto segregation in those days continuing after death.

We arrived at our section for the day, and unloaded the machines. Speedy stayed on the truck. Bud was going to take him to trim the Benedum mausoleum.

"Champ's goin' to do Mr. Benedum's," Bing blurted out. His voice was loud and whiny.

"CHAMP OF THE WORLD!" he screamed as Bud drove off with Speedy.

Carl explained to me that Speedy used to be a boxer. I asked if he was some kind of champion. "No," he laughed. "He's just a punch-drunk old bum."

We had five mowers: three were regular push power mowers. The other two were a big red Toro and a huge, self-propelled green machine called "Big Green." Carl took Big Green. He assigned Bill the Toro. He showed me how to use one of the push mowers – it was simple. He explained to me that Bing only used one of the simple push mowers, since that was all he could handle. We had gasoline cans with us, and filled up the tanks on our mowers. As Bing filled his, he gulped repeatedly as if he were drinking the gas. Carl explained that Bing thought he was a power mower. "Wait till you hear him," he laughed.

Carl assigned each of us a section, except Bing.

"I'll put Bing over there," he pointed, "…where he can't fuck anything up."

He talked to us about Bing in front of him like he wasn't there.

"CAPTAIN CARL!" Bing screamed as he strode off pushing his mower. The mower held him upright to a degree. When he walked without it he leaned pretty far forward. As he began mowing he started a loud, steady, high-pitched whine. The other guys looked at me and laughed.

"I told you he thinks he's a power mower," Carl explained. "He's nuts. He's been in the insane asylum." I wasn't sure if he was kidding or not.

From my section I could hear Bing singing along, imitating the power mower. To my amazement, he kept it up for hours, stopping only when the mower stopped. Carl enjoyed my reaction. It seemed like a fun place to work, with Bing as the entertainment.

At noon Bud picked us up for lunch. We left the mowers on site. We would return at one p.m. On the way back to the shed, we passed an elderly man in black pants, a long sleeve blue shirt, and suspenders. He wore a big black bowler hat that made him look oddly foreign. He held a broom that he used to sweep around the big building near the Dallas gate that housed the crematorium. Bing, leaning forward in a stupor, sprung to life when he saw the old man.

"GRAND OLD MAN! IVAN P. – GRAND OLD MAN!" he screamed.

Ivan just shook his broom at Bing.

We picked up Speedy at the mausoleum. "CHAMP OF THE WORLD!" Bing greeted him. Speedy didn't acknowledge him.

It felt good to sit down and relax after pushing the power mower for nearly four hours. We sat under a willow tree in a grass field near "the shed," which housed lots of different machinery and supplies. My mother had packed a lunch of sandwiches, an apple, and a can of pop, which I retrieved from the refrigerator in the shed and devoured quickly. We had an hour for lunch, so I leaned against the tree and rested. Bing, reading the paper, exclaimed, "The sheet metal workers got a raise of a dollar sixty an hour! That's more than what we make, Speedy!" Bing seemed to address everything to Speedy. He was right. I was paid minimum wage, $1.40 an hour, while Bing and Speedy, permanent employees, made $1.41.

That afternoon I learned the "Seven Points of Bingism." Crazy Bing had his own imaginary world of which he was the head – "Emperor Bing" – and enforced his rule with "Bing Troopers." He administered his "seven point" program to his enemies. Carl had him recite it to me. For each point he dramatically slapped his index finger against his open palm.

"Number one: shocked to insensibility with a million volts of lightning.

"Number two: head shaved.

"Number three: brains cut out.

"Number four: head cut off.

"Number five: cremated.

"Number six and seven: ashes frozen dry and shipped to the nearest star."

Carl and the others laughed heartily during the performance.

Bing also claimed that he had boiled many of the Pirates and Steelers in "HFO," or "hot fuckin' oil." He had a fascination with cremation and would at times interrupt his power mower whine to yell "CREMATION" or "HFO" for no apparent reason. When he yelled "CREMATION" he would snap his fingers next to his ear.

Bing's most elaborate fantasy was the Homewood Cemetery football team, nicknamed "Leaf Machine University." He imagined a team that included Bud as the coach, Carl as the quarterback, and Bing himself as the owner. Ivan, the "Grand Old Man," was the fullback and star player. We all had a position on the team. I was added as a defensive lineman. The team played on Tuesday nights, so every Wednesday Bing told us the details of the previous night's game. We opened with local rival Smithfield, a small cemetery across the street. We beat them 100-0, with Ivan scoring many touchdowns. As the season progressed we played other cemeteries from the Pittsburgh area, including our main rivals, Allegheny Cemetery. We won all the games by huge scores, in the eighties or nineties, with Ivan doing most of the scoring. We defeated Forest Lawn of Los Angeles by 40-0, setting up the final game of the year against powerhouse Arlington National. Bing talked about the game all week, building it up like it was the Super Bowl. He would get excited every time he saw Ivan, yelling "Arlington National," and "Grand Old Man." That Wednesday Bing explained what had happened in the game Tuesday night. We held our own in a valiant struggle against a bigger, stronger team, a scoreless tie until the final play, when Ivan scored on a fifty-yard touchdown run as time expired. We won, 7-0. Many times that day Bing shook his head in admiration and yelled "Grand Old Man!" The Grand Old Man had come through when it counted. When Bing tried to tell Ivan about it, Ivan motioned with his broom as if he were sticking it up Bing's ass.

During that summer I met several more characters, including "Diamond Jim," the cremator. Jim was a tall, older black man with light brown skin and "conked" salt-and-pepper hair that lay in soft waves. He had a big gold tooth in front that gleamed when he smiled. How ironic that he had such a blatant tooth, because he would often show us teeth left over from a cremation. When a cremation was underway, bluish-white smoke poured from the top of the crematorium and could be seen over most of the cemetery, letting all know what was going on, much like St. Peter's Basilica at the election of a pope. Bing would scream "CREMATION!

CREMATION!" when he saw the smoke. The odor was unlike anything I have ever smelled; not unpleasant, just strong and distinct.

The Superintendent was Jack McCoubrie, who Bing called "Uncle Jack". It wasn't a term of affection. McCoubrie had thick gray hair and a gray goatee. He always wore black dress pants and a short-sleeved white dress shirt. He was antagonistic to the workers, often sneaking up on us in his car to see if we were working. He would suddenly appear around a corner and slow down, glaring. Bing often warned, "Watch out for your Uncle." Bing was afraid of him, but said he was a lot better than the previous boss, "Uncle Sabin." Sabin was dead, but Bing and Speedy still despised him. When we passed his grave, a stark stone labeled "Sabin G. Bolton," Bing and Speedy would urinate on it. They often held their bladders until we were near Sabin's grave. Carl told me the story of how Speedy had once shit on Sabin's grave, only to wipe himself unknowingly with poison ivy. Both Bing and Speedy felt that Sabin cursed them from the grave, the poison ivy being evidence of this.

One day a severe storm hit, with thunder and lightning and heavy rain. We tried to take shelter under a tree. Bing panicked and ran to a nearby mausoleum, pounding on the front door. "UNCLE SABIN! UNCLE SABIN!" he screamed. "I'M SORRY I PISSED ON YOUR GRAVE! I'M SORRY SPEEDY SHIT ON YOUR GRAVE! SAVE ME! O SAVE ME UNCLE SABIN!"

The outburst appeared to be sincere, as Bing was obviously in great distress and near tears. Carl laughed uncontrollably, enjoying another crazy moment with Bing.

I learned the cemetery songs, which had been created by Carl. The first was to the tune of the Marine Corps song "From the Halls of Montezuma." Its first two lines were clever, but the lyrics deteriorated after that. We sang:

From the halls of the crematorium to the spires of old Homewood Gate.
We will cut our cemetery's grass, too little and too late.
First to have our ashes frozen dry and shipped to the nearest star,

We are proud to fight the battles of the Bing Government.

For the second song Carl assigned Bing the number "one," himself "two," and a third worker "three."

To the tune of "As the Caissons Go Rolling Along" we sang:

Over hill, over dale, we will hit the dusty trail,

As the power mowers go rolling along.

Up and down, in and out, counter march and left about,

As the power mowers go rolling along.

For it's high high he, in the cemetery,

Shout out your numbers loud and strong! ONE! TWO! THREE!

And the work you see, is done by two and three,

As the power mowers go rolling along.

Bing went along with it, shouting out "one" as the song mocked his work efforts.

Speedy was quiet, but after a few weeks he spoke with me. Upon hearing my name, he introduced himself as "Francis J. McMahon" and said, "I like you. You're Irish. We have to stick together."

He explained that he had been a teenage amateur boxer at 106 pounds. He got into the ring to spar with a 175 pounder and got seriously hurt. That was why his head jerked every ten seconds or so. He told me that Bing "lost his mind" on a Navy ship during the Korean War.

"That crazy Jew's been in seven different nuthouses. He goes to the VA Hospital every month for medicine and a checkup. He's nuts, but would never hurt anybody."

On rainy days we stayed in the shed and made "rough boxes," the cement vaults that held the caskets in the grave. This involved mixing the cement and pouring it into a mold. When it set, the rough box was ready. Bing called this activity "RBI School," which stood for "Rough Box Institute."

A skinny, wiry guy named "Ron the Gravedigger" operated the backhoe that dug the graves. In preparation for a funeral, we laid a rough box in a freshly dug grave. We erected a tent over the grave and put green carpets on the ground for the mourners to walk on. After it was over, we took down the tent and carpets.

By August I was a veteran grass cutter, and had made new friends of various ages. I went with Carl and Bill to an under 21 dance hall several times. They were nineteen and I was seventeen, but they let me "tag along." Carl asked a lot of different girls to dance. If they refused, he said he was "shot down." He kept track of how many times he was successful or "shot down." He loved to dance to "A Thousand Stars in the Sky" by Kathy Young and the Innocents.

I never forgot the characters or songs of that summer, and always remembered the "Seven Points of Bingism." The following year I went away to college. Carl joined the Marines at the height of the Vietnam War. While at college I saw an article about him in the Pittsburgh Press. He had been killed in a fire fight in Vietnam. I cut out his picture from the article, and kept it in my wallet for years. I have no doubt that Carl was a great soldier and comrade, laughing his way through the hardships of war.

Bing and Speedy worked there for years afterwards, making one cent above minimum wage. I ran into Speedy at a pub in Regent Square a few years after I had left. I asked how everyone was, and brought up the tragedy of Carl's death. He froze, silent for a long, awkward minute. Tears ran down the gray stubble of his cheek. He tried to talk, staring into his beer, the words not coming.

"I didn't even go to the funeral home," he said finally, his voice choking. "I know I should have... but I can't handle that stuff."

He turned away, embarrassed, again staring into his beer for what seemed like a long time. His head jerked, the legacy of his boxing injury. I wanted to comfort him.

"It's all right," I told him. "Carl would understand."

I believed it. His head jerked again.

THE END